"He's a lobo. A bad one, with a rep he's proud of. You don't give a gent like him the chance to start up with you. You got to draw on such a gent afore he issues you the invite. So slide out of my line of fire, sort of casual. I already got my gun out. But you're in my way."

Munro insisted, "You can't. You're talking crazy. They'd hang you sure for gunning a man with no reason at all, you idjet."

The stranger across the saloon called out, "You two, at that table, are you talking about me?"

Munro turned in his chair with a polite smile to reply, "As a matter of fact, we was."

THE GRASS OF GOODNIGHT

Lou Cameron

FAWCETT GOLD MEDAL • NEW YORK

A Fawcett Gold Medal Book
Published by Ballantine Books
Copyright © 1987 by Lou Cameron

Library of Congress Catalog Card Number: 87-90837

ISBN 0-449-13183-1

Manufactured in the United States of America

First Edition: September 1987

CHAPTER ONE

WYOMING TERRITORY, OCTOBER 21, 1878 . . .
They found what was left of Walking Fox four hours after
sunrise. The body lay faceup and appeared to be floating on
a rolling sea of sun-cured grass. Two arrow shafts rose side
by side from the breast of the dead scout's army-issue
greatcoat. But they hadn't lifted the hair Walking Fox, a
Pawnee, wore along the crest of his side-shaven skull.

Sergeant Mingis Munro halted the patrol fifty yards away
and dismounted to move in afoot. He circled the body
twice, searching for signs in the ankle-deep and wire-tough
shortgrass. He didn't spot any. He hadn't expected to. But
he knew he was expected to try.

He moved closer, dropped to one knee, and took a stiff
right wrist in his gauntleted hand. He lifted the arm, saw the
sleeve was still damp where it had been in contact with the
sod, and let it fall back there as he muttered, "They got you
before the sun was high enough to burn off the morning
frost. So they had time to whittle you religious. But they
never did. I suspicion there could be more to your demise
than you're letting on, old son."

1

Munro stared soberly at the arrow shafts. They didn't quite match. But both were vaned with raven feathers and banded with red and black medicine paint. He'd have felt better had even one been banded with blue. He knew the heads were barbed as well as driven deep. So he broke them off and tucked both in his boot top before he rose and called out, "Kellerman, front and center." When the shorter and somewhat older Corporal Kellerman joined him, Munro said, "Break out a tarp and have him lashed atop one of the ammo mules."

Kellerman frowned and asked, "We're taking this fool Indian with us, Sarge?"

Munro said, "We are. This man's army ain't in the habit of leaving its own behind, red, white, or black. So get to it. I mean to move out in less than five." Then he strode back to where his guidon rider was holding the reins of his mount for him. He didn't look back as Kellerman shouted, "Davis, Ryan, and Zuber, on the double!"

Munro took the reins with a nod of thanks and forked himself into the saddle. As he did so, a stray gust of prairie breeze with snow on its breath fluttered the nearby guidon and spooked his chestnut gelding. Munro steadied it with a firm but gentle hand. The guidon rider shot an uneasy glance up at the flapping red and white linen and opined, "If it was up to me, we'd consider casing our colors this close to Mister Lo, the poor Indian."

But Munro said, "It ain't up to you, or even me. The book says we got to display our colors on the offensive lest Mister Lo mistake us for a Sunday school outing."

The guidon rider grimaced and said, "I know what the book says. The trouble with fighting Indians by the book is that none of the red rascals have ever *read* it."

Munro shrugged and replied, "I've noticed that. But if illiteracy was the answer, they'd have won by now. I can't say I buy every A.R. total. But I've seen men ignore the book and still get run over by Mister Lo. It must have felt embarrassing as well as painsome, at the last."

He turned in his saddle to see how Kellerman and his detail were making out with the body. He saw they were lashing the tarp-wrapped Walking Fox facedown atop the ammo aboard one of their two pack mules. Another trooper facing another way called out, "Rider coming in from the south, Sarge. Looks like that breed, Kiowa Culhane."

Munro turned and, sure enough, saw Senior Scout Culhane coming at a mile-eating lope aboard a lathered paint pony. "Senior" was the war department's polite way of designating a white civilian contracted to scout for its Indian-fighting army. Munro knew the buckskin-clad Culhane only appeared sort of Indian because he wore his black hair long and dressed more Indian then most Indians attached to the army these days.

As Culhane reined in to join them he said, "I see the shavetail let you have half the platoon to play with, kid. You can save me riding all the way back to the post if you got any sand in your craw."

Munro didn't like to be called a kid, even by a fellow Texan. He knew he'd be old enough to vote by the time this hitch was up, and in a peacetime army where fifty-year-old captains were not at all rare, he figured they'd have never issued him his three stripes if they hadn't considered him grown-up enough to matter. But he knew it was a waste of time to argue the point with a man who was at least ten years his senior and inclined to glory in a total lack of military courtesy. So he replied, "I got as much sand as I might need. What have you got as might call for it?"

Culhane said, "I just found Dull Knife. The old Cheyenne devil is camped with his band less than an hour's ride

3

from here. Who's wrapped in that tarp back yonder, by the way?"

Munro said, "Walking Fox, one of the Pawnee attached to I&R. We just found him arrowed. It didn't read Cheyenne. Are you sure we're talking about a Cheyenne camp?"

Culhane snorted in disgust and asked, "Who else would be out here, off the reserves, at this late date, *Eskimo*? Dull Knife's band is the only one running loose this fall, kid."

He pointed south with an expansive sweep of his fringed sleeve as he added, "I know the draw they're holed up in. It's well down out of the wolf wind, with water and cottonwood. But it's narrow and steep-walled as well. So they won't have their lodges in a circle. They'll be strung out along the draw like a domino row, and so, do we work around unstream and charge down the draw stirrup to stirrup, we ought to be able to Sand Creek the sons of bitches good!"

Munro frowned and said, "Sand Creek was before my time, and I've always felt sort of good about that. That was the time we wiped out the wrong band of Indians, wasn't it?"

Culhane looked disgusted and said, "It ain't possible to wipe out the wrong Indians. They let Black Kettle get away at Sand Creek. They was only militia, not regular army. So when the Seventh Cav caught up with that same poor harmless cuss, right at the Washita, he was holding three white gals captive just to prove how innocent he was. One of the gals the Seventh rescued from the Cheyenne at the Washita is still locked up in an insane asylum back east. She'd no doubt testify how much she admired Mister Lo, the poor Indian, if she could do anything but stare at the walls of her padded cell and drool."

Munro knew Culhane had even more personal reasons for

hating Indians. So he said, "Let's not worry about long-dead Cheyenne. I have eighteen gun hands here to work with, counting you and me. The last report he had on Dull Knife gives him seventy or eighty braves and mayhaps twice that many dependents."

Culhane shrugged and said, "That's likely why they issue you boys repeating carbines and six-shooters. Of course, if four to one odds strikes you as too big a boo—"

Munro cut in to ask, "Were you aiming to show us where that camp might be, or are we just supposed to guess?"

Culhane laughed and said, "I heard you was from Texas, kid. So let's go *git* the damned old renegade!"

Munro glanced back, saw his troopers were as ready to move out as they'd ever be, and raised his free gauntlet to shout, "Column of twos, for'd hhhyo!" as he spurred his mount into an uncomfortable but sustainable trot. Riding at his left side as the guidon rider dressed on Munro's right, Culhane groaned, "Sweet Jesus, this ain't no way for a white man to ride, kid. I thought you was brung up cow, like me."

Munro said, "My kin had a stock spread on the Brazos. I had to learn to ride all over again after I joined up during the big Sioux rising. A cowhand enjoys the luxury of a fresh mount every morning. A trooper has to keep his one critter going day after day, and you may have noticed our two species don't share the same notions of comfort. That Indian pony you've been abusing ain't up to much more loping for a spell in any case."

Culhane swore and muttered, "Thank Gawd it ain't far, then. For I doubt my balls could stand much more army duty. You're bearing a mite wide to the east. Swing west a tad and you'll see their camp haze soon enough."

Munro frowned thoughtfully at the horizon ahead as he

5

asked, "Would a band on the dodge have their lodge fires lit this late in the day, Kiowa?"

Culhane said, "Did Dull Knife have any brains, he'd have never jumped the reserve this late in the year to begin with. I know they shouldn't be sending up smoke. You know they shouldn't be sending up smoke. But if they hadn't been sending up smoke, I'd have never spotted 'em, would I?"

Munro was silent for a couple of bounces. Then he said, "I dunno, Kiowa. That particular band has been doing something right if it's worked its way this far north from the Fort Reno reserve since September with so many of us looking to cut 'em off from their old stomping grounds. Is that smoke you saw all we're really talking about, or did you really spot one whole Cheyenne in the flesh?"

Culhane snorted in disgust and replied, "I value my hair too much to drop in for breakfast with knowed hostiles. I was out in the open like a big-ass bird when I spotted their camp haze and lit out to report the same. But, like I said, there ain't no other Indians but Cheyenne running loose in these parts no more."

Munro reached down with his free hand and drew one of the arrow shafts he'd broken off the dead Pawnee's chest out of his boot top. He passed it across to Culhane. The older and supposedly more experienced Indian fighter looked it over, passed it back, and said, "Sioux. It was *made* by a Sioux, I mean. But not around here. Sioux never hunted this far south, even when they was allowed to stay out late."

Munro said, "I know. In their Shining Times this stretch of the High Plains was disputed with considerable heat by Cheyenne and Crow. But the only noticable difference between Sioux and Crow is that they hate one another intense. So why couldn't we be talking about Crow arrows?"

Culhane said, "That's easy. The Crow are friendlies. They had the sense to side with us against the whole Lakota Confederacy during the big scare of Seventy-six."

Munro nodded but said, "I still don't think Walking Fox was killed by Cheyenne. They didn't mutilate his bow fingers. If a Cheyenne was in a hurry, he might not take a scalp. But he'd just never leave a dead enemy with his bow fingers intact. They have it on good authority that sickness is caused by ghost arrows shot by dead enemies left in any position to do so, see?"

Culhane grimaced and said, "Don't lecture your elders on such Indian notions, kid. Who but a hostile Cheyenne would want to kill one of our tame Pawnee?"

Munro said, "Just about any Crow who got the chance. It's true that the Crow are on our side when it comes to fighting Sioux. But whether the Crow like to admit it or not, they talk the same lingo and use the same medicine as their Sioux cousins. When they weren't fighting one another, in their Shining Times, the one thing Crow and Sioux agreed on was that *neither* could abide Pawnee. So try her this way. Say Walking Fox bumped noses, by the dawn's early light or darker, with a couple of Crow. Say said Crow just done what come natural when they spotted that Pawnee scalp roach, and then, when they moved in to count coup, they spotted his army-blue greatcoat and reconsidered. The Crow are supposed to be on our side. They'd have felt sort of chagrined when they saw they'd killed an army scout, even if he *was* a Pawnee, see?"

Culhane shook his head and said, "What in thunder would a band of Crow be doing in these parts, kid?"

Munro said, "Just about anything they had a mind to. Thanks to having sided with us during the big Sioux rising, Crow enjoy more privileges from the BIA than former hostiles these days. This is old Crow hunting ground. What

Indian agent would report 'em out of line if they just told him they was riding off for some fall hunting?"

Culhane thought about it as they rode on a spell. Then he said, "Well, whoever killed Walking Fox, they're out of line now. So I fail to see any real difference, no matter *who* we find camped in that draw I'm leading you boys to attack."

Munro shook his head wearily and said, "It's a good thing I'm in command of this patrol, then. I'm really not up to explaining an attack on a friendly band to a board of inquiry."

Culhane pointed back down the column at the distant bouncing bundle aboard the ammo mule as he snorted in disgust and asked, "Do you call what they done to that scout *friendly*?"

Munro said, "Not hardly. Even if it was an honest mistake, we have to take at least one of their young men in to stand trial for it. If I've put it together right, by now the elders will be expecting us, and they'll understand the way things just have to be." He rose in his stirrups for a better look as he spotted a faint blue haze ahead. Then he nodded and said, "They'd have put out their fires long before now if they were expecting to make a fight of it."

Culhane said, "Hold on, kid. You can't just ride in like a big-ass bird. We got to swing around and come down the draw at 'em with some cover working for us."

But Munro said, "That would make 'em think we were out to Sand Creek 'em for sure." Then he turned in his saddle to shout, "Line of skirmish to my rear at pistol range." He added to his guidon rider, "Drop back with Kellerman and let them dress on you."

As the guidon rider fell back, Culhane swore and said, "It was nice knowing you, kid. But I signed a scouting contract with the army, not a suicide pact. Even if you ain't

8

offering yourself to Cheyenne on a silver platter, what makes you so sure any Crow chief would rather see one of his own die than you?"

Munro shrugged and said, "Like the old song says, farther along, we'll know more about it."

Culhane didn't answer. He was already dropping back to line up abreast with the others. Munro was mildly surprised to notice how much he missed his company. But he knew this was the way it was supposed to be done. Even if he was wrong and the Indians camped in the draw ahead were Cheyenne, nine times out of ten they'd prefer to hear what a man alone on point had to say before they made any hostile moves.

But as he rode closer, out ahead of his men, he learned, too late, that this was to be the tenth time. He didn't see the one who arrowed him. He just felt the numbing blow and stared down in dull wonder at the arrow embedded in his chest. As he swayed sickeningly in his saddle, with the sky above turning ruby-red, he could see the arrow in him wasn't Cheyenne, either. As he fell from his saddle, he wondered idly why this should seem at all important. Then he hit the ground and didn't wonder anything at all for quite some time.

CHAPTER TWO

The next time Mingis Munro opened his eyes it was snowing outside. His iron-bound cot was right under a window, and the snow was scratching like a kitten at the panes. He wished he was out there in the blizzard. He was hot and sweaty as hell. He tried to sit up. Someone stabbed him in the chest with a rusty dagger, and he groaned aloud and lay back, trying not to breathe so hard. For some fool reason his left forearm was strapped tightly to his chest with bandages and tape. It itched ferociously.

A nursing sister who'd heard him groan came over to his cot to stare down in mock severity and tell him to be a good boy and lie still. She was young and pretty. So he didn't cuss her. He licked his dry lips and asked where he was and how come.

She said, "You've had quite a bad time, Sergeant. We were afraid we'd lost you before the fever broke a few hours ago. Are you thirsty? You should be."

He said, "I could drink at least a river, and if I'm getting *over* a fever, I'd hate to feel the real thing. How long was I out, Sister?"

She said, "Three days and four nights. Don't go away. I'll fetch you some water."

He wiped his sleep-gummed face with his free hand as his head began to clear a bit more. The nursing sister was back almost at once with a tin cup of the best water he'd ever tasted. As he drained the cup and asked for more, she dimpled and told him, "Not until the regimental surgeon looks you over, Sergeant. I was told to tell him the moment you opened your eyes. So why don't you just relax, and I'll have him here in a jiffy."

But as she turned away, he croaked, "Wait! What about my men? Did anyone else make it?"

She hesitated before she told him. "I'm afraid poor Corporal Kellerman was killed and trooper Davis was wounded, albeit not as severely as yourself. Otherwise, I hear it was a one-sided victory."

"Against who? Were we fighting Crow or Cheyenne?"

She said, "Crow, of course. I surely don't have to tell *you*, of all people, that at least that one band of Crow was on the warpath, the ungrateful brutes."

Then she left. A million years went by as Munro lay alone in what had to be some sort of emergency ward. Then she was back with a fatherly-looking gent with a white smock on over whatever kit he wore under it. Munro couldn't tell if he was an officer or one of the civilian surgeons attached to the post. It was probably safer to sir him in either case.

The surgeon felt Munro's forehead and took his pulse before he opined. "Well, sometimes we're wrong. I guess you know you really should be dead right now, don't you, son?"

Munro grinned up weakly and replied, "No excuse, sir. How soon should I be fit for duty again?"

The older man looked out the window as if he was

wondering when the snow would let up as he answered soberly, "You strike me as a grown man, Sergeant. So I won't shilly-shally. You won't be returning to duty in this man's army. Ever. You'll be due an honorable discharge and all pay and allowances coming to you, of course, but—"

"Hold on!" Munro cut in, protesting, "I was only grazed with a durned old arrow. I still got all my arms and legs and such, don't I?"

The surgeon said, "You do, and in a few short weeks you ought to be up and about, feeling fit as a fiddle. But you see, you've lost your left lung. That arrow collapsed it, which was bad enough. Then the wound mortified. So we just had to take your infected lung out, and you still barely made it. It was a good thing you were so young and healthy when they put that dirty arrow in you, Sergeant. But as I said, you'll hardly notice it once you get your strength back."

Munro inhaled experimentally and insisted, "I hardly notice it right now. How come I can breathe if I only got one lung?"

The older man explained, "I just said you were in fine shape, otherwise. In times to come, you may notice some shortness of breath if you really push yourself. But you ought to be able to put in a full day's sensible work without noticing it."

"Then how come you don't think I'll be fit to soldier?" asked Munro. So the surgeon told him, not unkindly but flatly, "Because a soldier isn't supposed to put in a sensible day's work. He's supposed to push himself beyond common sense when he has to, and, well, you just won't be able to do that anymore, Sergeant."

He turned back to the nursing sister to say, "Bed rest and all the food and liquids he may want. Take his temperature now and again and notify me if it goes over a hundred."

The girl nodded and asked, "Is he free to receive visitors,

12

sir? Some of his friends have been out front, asking about him."

The surgeon nodded and said, "I don't expect another crisis. We simply have to keep him comfortable and let nature run its course now."

Then he left, not saying anything more to Munro. As if she'd read the wounded youth's mind, she came closer and bent over to confide, "He's not really treating you like a slab of beef, you know. He's a very kind man, inside."

Munro smiled thinly and said, "I reckon I'll have to take your word for it, then. He sure is good at hiding his tender feelings."

She said, "I know. I caught him crying in the scrub room after he lost Corporal Kellerman on the operating table."

Munro nodded soberly and said, "I stand corrected, then. But how in thunder did any of us wind up back here at the post to be operated on one way or the other?"

She said, "I don't know the details. Apparently, when both you noncoms went down, Senior Scout Culhane took command. I hear he's been put in for a citation. He must be awfully brave."

Munro frowned. "I'd have said crazy-mean, if I didn't seem to owe my life to him right now. How many prisoners did he bring in with the rest of us?"

She looked blank and asked, "Prisoners?"

He just nodded and said, "Dumb question. They say the real Kiowa wiped out his family, down in Texas, during the war between the states. He was riding for Texas back east at the time, of course. I doubt he took many Kiowa as prisoners during the first buffalo war on the Staked Plains, come to study on it."

She shrugged and said, "Well, those *Crow* were awfully mean to you boys the other day, too. I suppose he felt he had enough on his plate getting you all out of that treacherous ambush. He's been asking about you a lot, Sergeant. Shall I bring him in the next time he calls on you?"

Munro started to say no. Then he nodded and said, "Sure. Maybe he knows what in thunder happened out there. I know I surely don't."

So later that evening, as Munro was sitting up in bed eating some awful goo they said he had to have until his stomach woke up better, the pretty young gal brought the ugly and greasy scout in to visit her one patient.

Culhane pulled a bentwood chair over by Munro's cot and waited until the nursing sister left them alone together before he said, "Well, you was right about 'em being Crow, and I was right about the way to deal with the sons of bitches."

Munro said, "You might have spared the women and children at least."

Culhane looked incredulous and asked, "Why? She-male lice just breed more nits, and nits just grow up to be lice. How could you feel pity for a band that paid you back for your understanding nature with an arrow through your fool ribs, old son?"

Munro said, "I wasn't arrowed by women and children. I was arrowed at most by one man. Likely one of the hotheads as killed Walking Fox to begin with."

Culhane chuckled fondly and said, "Yeah. You *said* we'd have to bring him in. I reckon he didn't want to come."

"All right. I was too trusting. I recall being hit. What else happened, damn it?"

Culhane shrugged and said, "I ordered a charge, and we rid in shooting, of course."

Munro frowned and asked, "On whose authority? What was my second in comman doing while all this was going on?"

Culhane shrugged and replied, "He never said. We found

14

him on the ground near you, afterwards, and he never woke up to argue the chain of command. What was I supposed to do, suck my infernal thumb till some *Indian* told me what to do?"

Munro sighed and said, "It hardly matters, now. With everyone on the other side dead, I reckon we'll just never know how many of 'em were really resisting us."

"Hell, kid, they was *all* resisting by the time we finished off the last of 'em!"

Munro grimaced and said, "That's no doubt how you licked 'em so good with such light casualties, then. I said it hardly matters now. But meanwhile, has anyone ever seen hide or hair of the Indians we were sent out to look for?"

Culhane nodded and said, "The news just come over the wire from Camp Robinson. Dull Knife and his frostbit Cheyenne just got cornered near the Nebraska line, and he's surrendered again. You'd think by now even Dull Knife would find that tedious. But if he really means it this time, me and you could have a real problem to worry on, kid."

Munro said, "What are you talking about? If Dull Knife has gone out of business, there isn't an important fighting chief left to worry about in these parts."

Culhane glanced around as if to make sure they weren't being overheard before he leaned closer and confided, "That's just it. President Hayes has been cutting military spending something scandalous, even with Mister Lo still acting up. With the Lakota Confederacy cowed and scattered, that penny-pinching damnyankee is sure to whittle the War Department even closer to the bone, and my scouting contract comes up for renewal at the end of the year."

Munro smiled thinly and said, "My heart bleeds for you. I believe I liked you better when I thought you just butchered Indians because you hated them."

Culhane shrugged and asked, "Where in the U.S. Constitution do it say a man can't combine business with pleasure? You may not feel so smug about your steadier job with Uncle Sam once you see how slow promotions come your way in a stripped-down army."

Munro laughed bitterly and said, "I may be out of a job before you are. They just told me I'll be facing a medical discharge as soon as I'm up and about again, and I'll be damned if I mean to lie slugabed, eating gruel, through Christmas."

Culhane brightened and replied, "You won't be. That purdy gal out front told me you figure to be out of bed in no more'n one month. She never told me they was fixing to boot you out of the army, though. What are you planning to take up next, seeing as they won't let you soldier no more, kid?"

Munro shrugged his one good shoulder and said, "I've only had a few hours to study on that. But I reckon I'll just have to go back down to Texas and take up where I left off, with cows."

Culhane looked disgusted and said, "That ain't no job for a white man. I'd swamp saloons afore I'd go back to being a cowhand. It's all work, no play, and damned little pay, as I recall from my misspent youth afore the war."

Munro nodded and said, "I noticed. That's why I joined up when I turned eighteen and found myself riding drag again on the same day. But I dunno, Kiowa. In the last three years I've found my fool self doing lots of things I didn't really want to. I thought I was signing up for a life of travel and adventure. But travel can get tedious when it's mostly patrolling the same old prairie, and to tell the truth I've found killing Indians and vice versa more disgusting than adventurous. Working cows may not be much of an adventure. But there's been many a night on the trail I've

16

looked back on my old trade with a certain fondness, and, hell, it ain't as if I had any *other* trade."

Culhane said, "You're wrong. You've larnt skills in the army they just don't teach on any cattle spread, kid. You know how to handle a gun. You've been in more than one dirty fight and come out alive. How many men do you reckon there are who can say, for sure, they stand ready to battle it out with bullets, not fists? There's a kid in every schoolyard who's willing to fight with his fool fists. But it's the part about bullets as separates the men from the boys. This world is filled with roughnecks. But real gunfighters are scarce as hen's teeth, and, like anything else that's scarce, real gunfighters are in considerable demand, see?"

Munro shook his head and said, "If you're suggesting I take up assassination as a trade, forget it. It's always bothered me a mite to blow away Indians even if they were out to do the same to me. I got less respect for a hired gun than I have for an honest pimp. So once I get my strength back, I'll just have to see if I remember how to rope and hog-tie as good as I used to. I was almost a top hand in my teens, you know, and they say a top hand can demand as much as a dollar and a half a day since the price of beef has started to rise back east, with the depression over at last."

Culhane insisted, "It'll always be a job for kids and niggers. I wasn't talking about hiring out as a paid killer, damn it. Do I look like an infernal murderer?"

Munro was too polite to answer truthfully. So he asked Culhane to get to the point.

The older fighting man said, "If they fail to renew my scouting contract, I figure I might sign on as some sort of armed guard or range detective. Regular lawmen don't get paid all that much. But the private agencies pay as much as a hundred a month for an experienced gun hand."

Munro shook his head and said, "You're dreaming. I

17

know an old boy who works as an armed guard for the Union Pacific, and he was sort of bragging when he told me he drew six bits a day and all the dining car food he wanted. Like I just said, a top hand can do better than that."

Culhane shrugged and said, "Well, they pay more for what you might call a specialist or troubleshooter."

"Do tell? How much trouble do they expect you to shoot for real money?"

"Such trouble as the regular guards can't handle," Kiowa Culhane said as he got to his feet and shoved the chair back where he'd found it. He added, "We can talk about it on the way back to Texas if we both get run off this post around New Year's. You do want me to ride back to Texas with you, don't you, kid?"

Munro relied, "I hadn't got around to thinking on how I meant to get home yet, and to tell the truth I don't know if I'd want the company of a man who keeps calling me a kid."

Culhane nodded soberly down at him and said, "That sounds fair. I admire you because I know you got sand in your craw, and we'd both be safer traveling all that way through Yankee country side by side. I won't call you a kid no more if it upsets you. What do you like to be called if I can't call you kid?"

Munro sighed and said, "My folk named me Mingis. Don't ask me why, and I can't say I like it all that much. But it is my name."

Culhane nodded and said, "All right, from now on I'll just call you Mingo, and we'll study more on our future careers once we find out if and when we're off to Texas together."

He started to turn away. Then he said, "I can get you something to drink or smoke at the suttler's, if you think that nursing gal might let me. She's a mighty purdy little thing. I sure could use some of that right now."

Munro scowled and said, "I can send for my own tobacco as soon as they tell me I can have it. So don't bother the gal, either way. I mean that, Kiowa."

Culhane laughed and said, "Hell, I won't mess with her if you got first dibs on her, Mingo. Me and you is fixing to be pards, see?"

Munro didn't see. But when Culhane held out a friendly hand, Munro was willing to shake so they could part polite. Then he finished his bowl of gruel and forgot about it. He had no idea when, or how, he meant to get back to Texas. But he knew he had no intention of traveling that far in the company of such a pain in the ass.

CHAPTER THREE

Munro was up and about by Thanksgiving, but they wouldn't let him go anywhere. He still felt a little giddy when he first got out of bed in the morning, and he couldn't tell how much of his strength he might have recovered, since all he got to do was mope about the dayroom in canvas slippers and a hospital robe. Miss Billie, the nursing sister, fussed at him every time she caught him with the robe open, despite the way they overheated the base hospital. She said a lot of winter agues were going around and that it was better to feel a might sweaty than be dead. When he could get away from her in the shower room, he could see that his chest scar looked less disgusting every day. It still hurt a mite if he expanded his ribs all the way and swung his left arm over his head. But that was his rein arm and not his throwing arm, so what the hell.

By Christmas he felt fully recovered. But the surgeon made him do a mess of deep knee bends, listened to his breathing with a stethoscope, and wanted to keep him at least six weeks into 1879.

The finance officer came to Munro's rescue in the

interests of neat bookkeeping and economy. The day before New Year's they gave him his discharge papers, three months' back pay, and six cents a mile traveling allowance to get him home to Texas. A soldier being mustered out rated one full-dress uniform lest he have to leave the post naked. But Munro still had the work duds he'd had on the day he'd joined up, along with his old boots and gun rig.

He'd been almost full grown when he passed his first physical, and he'd lost some weight recovering from his close call. So the pants fit about right, and his old hickory shirt was only a little tight. He'd taken his personal Colt '74 out to clean and oil once a month all the time he was in service. So he knew it was in better shape than he was right now, even if it did ride sort of funny on his hip now that he was used to wearing his heavier army rig higher. He hadn't joined up in midwinter, so he kept his army-issue greatcoat, put on his old gray Stetson, and caught a ride to the nearest railhead with the mail wagon headed that way before noon.

He'd promised to say good-bye to Miss Billie and the other boys in her ward. But he knew she was just friendly by nature, and he had a long ride ahead of him. He wasn't good at good-byes in any case. The mail wagon driver let him take turns with the reins, but it was still a long, tedious trip into Medicine Wells.

The rolling prairie had gone to painted pony hide as it always did between serious snowfalls on the High Plains. The thin dry air didn't slow the sunlight much, even in winter. So all the south and west slopes lay tawny-brown as the last snow soaked into the ever-thirsty loam or simply sublimed away without melting. Smaller patches of dirty white snow remained and would remain in northeast-facing hollows well into the spring green up.

As they got closer to the railhead, Munro began to spot half-wild scattered cattle with familiar calico hides and horns too long for a sensible buffalo to want. When he commented on this to the driver, he was told, "Yeah, they've opened the Goodnight Trail again now that Mister Lo's been whupped good. You'll see Texas men as well as cows once we get closer to town. Watch your step in that Yankee-blue greatcoat until you can at least get rid of them yaller stripes, Sarge. I know the Reconstruction's over, and you know it's over. But some of them Texas boys still seem to want a rematch."

Munro smiled thinly and said, "I know how to get along with Texans. I just find it surprising to see Texas cows and such this far up in buffalo country."

The driver said, "You must not have been getting into Medicine Wells much lately. With both the buffalo and Indians about shot off, they're giving old Captain Goodnight's experiment another try. You've heard about Goodnight and Loving, haven't you?"

Munro said he had. But the driver had nothing better to talk about. So he said, "Captain Charlie Goodnight and his pard, old Oliver Loving, rounded up a swamping herd of unclaimed cattle running wild after the war between the states. Since others in Texas had the same notion, Goodnight and Loving found themselves crowded for grass and water."

Munro said, "I know. Both are hard to come by in west Texas."

The driver waved his whip hand at the horizon ahead and said, "As anyone can see, there's more grass and less thirsty weather as you work north. So Goodnight and Loving commenced to push their cattle, and their luck, into Indian country by the late '60s. They sold enough beef to the army at Fort Sumner to buy an even bigger herd. Oliver Loving was killed by Comanche on the next try. But old Goodnight invented the chuck wagon, gathered enough Texas gun slicks to scare any sensible Indians, and bulled ever north until he was selling beef all the way up in Montana."

Munro asked, "Didn't he settle on a Colorado home spread in the end?"

"So they say. You could herd beef up through serious Indian country, but you couldn't *hold* 'em long on Mister Lo's hunting ground. Goodnight even had to abandon his Colorado range and move back to Texas when the Arapaho throwed in with the Lakota Confederacy under Red Cloud. But as you may have noticed, we've put all the red rascals in their place, and all the grass Goodnight wanted for Texas cows is still here. I can't say where Goodnight himself might be right now. But his numerous admirers have been shoving Texas cattle up this way as fast as they can ride."

As they topped a rise to see the smoke haze and rooftops of Medicine Wells ahead at last, the driver spat and added, "If I was you, I'd cut them stripes off afore we reach the city limits. It's almost New Year's Eve, and the town will be crowded with unreconstructed rebels spoiling for fun."

Munro considered, shrugged, and said, "I'd have to take this coat off to do it right, and it's sort of nippy. I don't mean to be in town long enough for it to matter, anyways. I'll tend to it on the first train I can catch for warmer climes."

The driver didn't argue. As they drove into town, Munro saw Medicine Wells had grown some since the last time he'd wasted a three-day pass on such a tedious place.

Medicine Wells was named for the barely drinkable well water they'd had to drill for on this rise between the headwaters of the Cheyenne and Powder rivers, neither of which would have been considered a river in the wetter country east of the Big Muddy. The water they'd drilled for had been meant for the locomotives of the overoptimistic spur line laid during the railroading boom of the early '70s. The original promoters had gone bust in the crash of

'74, of course. But the bigger Burlington line had bought up the track to serve as a feeder spur, and so, although it called for some tedious transferring, one could still catch a train out of Medicine Wells three times a week. The timetable in Munro's breast pocket said there was a southbound combination pulling out just after sundown. So they'd made it with just an hour or so to spare.

Or so they thought. The mail driver was as sore as Munro when the stationmaster told them the schedule had been changed. He seemed to find it more important than they did that the line was now offering service *four* times a week, albeit not that evening.

As they walked back out to the muddy, rutted street, Munro told the driver, "The least I can do is buy you a drink, lest you feel the trip was a total waste."

But the driver shook his head and said, "No thanks. I'd as soon drink the old year out back at the post suttler's as in any of these infernal saloons after dark."

Munro said, "I need a decent hotel more than I need a saloon right now. Do you know of one, seeing as you know this town so well?"

The driver said, "I know it well enough to advise you to come back to the post with me on New Year's Eve, Sarge. There ain't no decent hotel. But the Bull Head, across the way to your left, is said to be a real hotel and not a whorehouse. More than that I can't tell you. Are you sure I can't talk you into coming back to the post for the night?"

Munro said, "I don't belong on any army post no more, and, no offense, that was one tedious ride, just going one way."

So they shook on it and parted friendly. Munro picked up his duffel and legged it over to the hotel he'd been advised to try. He noticed the entrance was right next to a saloon, from whence came the tinkle of a piano playing "Dixie,"

24

off-key. Munro sighed and went into the Bull Head. A skinny old gent behind the key counter shook his head at him and said, "We're full-up. Didn't anyone tell you this was New Year's Eve?"

Munro said, "They didn't even tell me the infernal train wasn't running tonight. How much it cost me to leave my duffel here with you, at least?"

The old-timer shook his head. Then he shot a thoughtful look at the sleeve of Munro's greatcoat and said, "Let's talk about the odd way you seem to be dressed, young feller. Are you a trooper or a cowboy?"

Munro said, "Neither. I just got mustered out, and I ain't got a job yet."

The old man nodded and said, "You never made three stripes as a guardhouse lawyer. How many Indians do you figure you civilized for us, Sergeant?"

Munro shrugged and asked, "Who counts? Can you recall just how many gals you might have kissed in your time, damn it?"

The old-timer laughed and said, "Yeah, you've seen the elephant, and some of us, at least, remember how glad we was to see you boys around here until mighty recently. You're in room 207. Here's your key. Now you got to give me a dollar because I just work here. If I owned the place it'd be on the house, soldier."

Munro said that sounded more than fair. He wasn't so sure once he was upstairs in the dinky, windowless cubby hole they glorified by calling a room. The brass bedstead took up most of the space, and the bed linens hadn't been changed in living memory.

He swore, tossed his duffel on the sagging mattress, and took off his army greatcoat. There was no door hook. He draped it over the foot of the bedstead. He started to take off his gun rig. But then he decided not to. It was early. He was

25

hungry. So he went back down to see if they served anything but "Dixie" in the saloon next door.

It was getting even colder as the sun went down. But it was only a few shirt-sleeved paces, and as he stepped inside, he was glad he'd left his coat behind for more than one reason. The red-hot potbellied stove in the center of the sawdust-covered floor had the place warmer and stuffier than it needed to be, and the gents bellied up to the bar looked sort of wild and woolly as well as Texan. Munro was looking for a spot he could edge into the bar without risking a fight when a familiar voice behind him called out, "Mingo! Over here, you old basser!"

He turned and didn't recognized the dark-suited figure seated alone at a corner table until it waved at him again. Then he saw it was Kiowa Culhane, dressed civilized and suffering the effects of a shave and haircut. Munro had no place better to go. So he went over, took the empty seat across from the erstwhile scout, and said, "I see you missed your rail connections south, too. They didn't renew your contract, huh?"

Culhane shrugged and said, "They'll regret it more than I will when Mister Lo thaws out this spring. I might have been held over another year had not some gent from the BIA made a fuss about that little scrape we had with his pet Crow. Do you know the son of a bitch had the nerve to accuse me of leading an attack on a friendly band with a BIA hunting permit?"

Munro said, "I figured they might. I come in here to see if I could get something to eat. How did you ever get that beer mug you're holding through that stampede at the bar?"

Culhane laughed and called out to a shamelessly dressed gal leaning against the upright piano as the professor played yet another refrain of the "Lost Cause." As she ambled over, Munro saw she was even uglier up close. But when

26

Culhane said, "Honey, this is a famished hero in need of grits and gravy," she smiled as friendly as a gal with no front teeth could manage and said she might be able to root out some ham and eggs. She asked Munro if he wanted draft or red-eye to wash it down with, and before he could answer, Culhane said, "Both. Bring us a bottle of rye and a pitcher of suds, and come morning I'll marry you, Trixie."

She laughed, said she wasn't the marrying kind, and left for the kitchen. Culhane chuckled fondly after her and said, "I mean to find out just what kind she is before the sun comes up on a new year, pard. Do you want me to ask her if she has a friend?"

Munro laughed and said, "Not hardly. She might not be as good-looking."

Culhane said, "Easy for you to say. I saw that handsome nurse you've been sparking all this time, Mingo. So fess up. How was she?"

Munro grimaced and replied, "I know you'll find this hard to believe, Kiowa, but there's something about having a gal change your bedpan and scrub your privates that just seems to take all the romance out of a relationship. Don't talk dirty about a gal as may have saved my life more than once and I won't talk dirty about the toothless love of your life, hear?"

Culhane laughed and said, "Don't knock kissing a gal with no front teeth till you've tried it. By the time you manage to live past thirty, you won't be so picky. I could tell you tales of pure desperation. But I wouldn't want to ruin your appetite, and what the hell, at least I can say I've never done it to anything that wasn't she-male, at least."

Trixie came back with a heavy tray that made Munro like her much better. As she bent over to spread the food and drink on the bare wood in front of him, Munro could tell she'd splashed on fresh violet water in the meantime. He

27

sincerely hoped she'd done so for Culhane. She'd sort of neglected her armpits.

Munro dug into the ham and eggs. They were surprisingly good. He scraped his plate clean and washed the last crumbs down with beer before he got to wondering why the piano had stopped. He saw Trixie had vanished as well and that more than one of the cowhands who'd been blocking access to the bar across the saloon seemed to be drifting out with the desperately casual movements of gents who neither wanted to stay nor look like they were just plain running.

Munro glanced at Culhane, who had a better view from his seat, and asked, "What's up?"

Culhane said quiety, "I ain't sure. There's a new customer who seems to have the center of the bar all to himself. I don't know him. Don't turn around. Whoever he is, he's on the prod. He's wearing two guns, low, in a fancy buscadero rig. Otherwise, he's dressed more like an undertaker. Tinhorn gambler, I reckon. He sure don't seem popular, whoever he is."

Munro's back began to itch. He muttered, "I was warned about New Year's Eve in a tough cow town. Does he look drunk?"

Culhane said, "Nope. Just mean. But what the hell, we're sort of mean, too. Do you want to ask him what's on his mind or shall I?"

Munro said, "Damn it, Kiowa, I only came in here for ham and eggs, not a war. Why don't we just pay up and leave? There's nothing here worth fighting over now that Trixie's lit out."

The barkeep no doubt would have liked to follow Trixie. But Munro heard a cold voice behind him snap, "Where do you think you're going, landlord? I told you I wanted a shot glass and a bottle of good Kentucky mash. So where's it at?"

Munro heard the sound of glass sliding across mahogany as an older and more timid voice replied, "Sure, Blacky. Anything you say. On the house."

Then Culhane murmured, "I wish I could get service like that. The old man's crawfishing back, and, yep, he just ducked out of sight entire. There's nobody now but us and this Blacky. Be ready to hit the sawdust as I make my own move, Mingo."

Munro protested. "Hold on. You can't just gun a man for drinking alone. So far he ain't done nothing to us, Kiowa."

Culhane said, "He will. There's nobody else left for him to do anything to, and I know that look on his face of old. He's a lobo. A bad one, with a rep he's proud of. You don't give a gent like him the chance to start up with you. You got to draw on such a gent afore he issues you the invite. So slide out of my line of fire, sort of casual. I already got my gun out. But you're in my way."

Munro insisted, "You can't. You're taking crazy. They'd hang you sure for gunning a man with no reason at all, you idjet."

The stranger across the saloon called out, "You two, at that table, are you talking about me?"

Munro turned in his chair with a polite smile to reply, "As a matter of fact, we was. Seeing as it's so quiet in here, and being it's New Year's Eve, I was wondering if you'd like to join us."

He could see now that Culhane had reason to describe the black-suited Blacky as spooky. But the dark hatchet-face man was smiling as replied, "Why, that sounds mighty neighborly of you, sonny. What's your name, and does your mother know you're out this late?"

Munro sighed and started to rise to his feet as, behind him, Culhane hissed, "No!"

And then things got confusing as hell for a spell.

Munro went for his own gun as the room filled with pungent blue smoke and the roar of gunfire. But by the time he had his Colt '74 in hand, it was over. The stranger called Blacky lay facedown in the sawdust with his own guns, still smoking, in both hands. Culhane was standing beside Munro, reloading, as he asked, "Where did he hit you, Mingo?"

Munro gasped and said, "Nowheres. What in thunder happened just now, Kiowa?"

Culhane said, "I told you I had him covered. He meant to get you on the rise. He should have. That was close as hell, Mingo. Don't ever act that foolish again."

"Jesus H. Christ! He had no call to gun me. How did you *know*?"

"I told you I'd seen his breed before. Did you really think a gun slick out to add to his rep would need a *reason* to kill, Mingo? How long do you think such a loco lobo would last if he issued engraved invites to a shoot-out?"

Munro gulped and said, "Well, that's twice I owe you. I reckon I just ain't got what it takes to be a gent like him, or you, for that matter."

Culhane said, "I know. He who hesitates in love is lost, and he who don't shoot first and ask questions later is dead. But the son of a bitch guessed wrong this time. So what say we get the hell out of here before the law shows up to ask pesky details?"

Munro protested, "We can't just light out and leave him like that without a word of explanation, Kiowa."

The older man holstered his gun and said, "Sure we can. I know where the back door is, and I got a room just up the alley. Come on. There was no witnesses, and I somehow doubt the rascal was all that popular."

Munro insisted, "We'd look guilty for sure if we did that."

"Hell, we *are* guilty. Leastways, I am. This is neither the time nor place to go by the book, old son. I for one mean to be long gone by the time the law arrives. Are you coming or ain't you?"

Munro looked uncertain. Culhane growled, "Suit yourself, you fool kid!" and headed for the kitchen.

He'd no sooner left when a weary-looking older man with a sawed-off shotgun called out from the front door, "Drop that pistol, cowboy. I don't mean to say it twice."

Munro realized he was in fact still standing over the body with his six-gun in hand. He let it fall to the floor and raised both empty hands as he called out, "Hold your fire. It ain't like it might look to you."

The older man came in, the lamplight gleaming on the muzzle of his scatter-gun and the brass star pinned to the breast of his sheepskin as he said, "You just step clear whilst I have a look at whatever you've wrought. It can't be Blacky Dawson at this late date but. . . . Son of a bitch, it *is*!"

The town marshal lowered the muzzle of his scatter-gun and called out the door, "It's all right, boys! Come on in and see what this young gent did to Blacky Dawson! I don't know *how* he did it, but the murderous maniac is dead as a turd in a milk bucket!"

Then he told Munro to pick up his gun and put it away, adding, "You'll have a hard time buying your own drinks in this town for a spell, son. You stand to collect a considerable bounty on the rascal as well."

Munro picked up his gun and started to explain. But by then the place was filled with joyous locals who insisted on literally picking him up and seating him on the bar as they babbled about how much they admired him. A deputy vaulted the bar and began to serve until the old barkeep came out of hiding and made him stop. When he, too,

31

learned what lay facedown on the far side of the bar, he let out a war whoop and announced all drinks were on the house.

As he handed a schooner of suds up to Munro, the confused youth managed to ask if it was safe to assume the late Blacky Dawson had done something nobody in town seemed to approve of.

Another local told him, "He was wanted for everything but the clap, son. He must have been out of his mind to come back here after robbing our bank last summer. But then, they always said he was mad-dog crazy!"

A bearded man asked Munro's name, adding that he meant to put it in the local paper. Munro introduced himself and tried to add that it had not been he who'd gunned the villainous Dawson. But his voice was lost in the thunderous applause as his questioner shouted, "His name is Mingis Munro, and I say three cheers for the same!"

It went on like that for quite a spell before things calmed down enough for the marshal to order the body taken to the town hall. He turned to Munro to explain. "You'd best come, too, son. They'll want you to pose with the body when they photograph it."

Munro hopped off the bar, saying, "You do me more honor than I deserve, gents." But before he could explain further, another noisy citizen came in to shout in outrage, "Somebody just stole my damned old horse!"

The town marshal shushed whatever Munro was about to say and turned to the outraged citizen to ask, "You mean that fine bay thoroughbred of your'n, Silas? Who'd be dumb enough to steal a horse so well knowed in these parts?"

The once called Silas answered loudly, "Some son of a bitch who's in a hurry, of course. Ain't another horse in this township as could catch my Brownie Boy, and I'll just bet the horse thief knows it!"

The marshal frowned thoughtfully and said, "Well, there ain't no train tonight, and anyone who came back here with Blacky Dawson would hardly see fit to hang about now that he's dead."

He turned back to Munro to ask, "What do you think, son? As our expert on the last movements of the late Black Dawson, would you hazard a guess as to whether he was riding alone or not?"

Munro was pretty sure he knew who'd lit out on the fastest mount he could find in a hurry. So he chose every word carefully as he opined, "It ain't for me to even guess at. I can't say I ever saw Dawson riding with or aboard anything. The first time I laid eyes on him was right here in this saloon just before it got so noisy."

The older man nodded approvingly and said, "I admire a modest young gent who sticks to just the facts he knows. I'm paid to guess more about such matters. So it's my considered opinion the outlaw come back here to do something dirty with at least one pard to back his play. Lucky for you, they weren't together when Blacky come in here and. . . . Say, how did you know it was right to gun him if you didn't know who he was, Munro?"

"I think it was mostly his notion to start the fight, sir."

"Well, you just proved you were better than one of the best. So no doubt his pard just lit out, scared skinny. There's no sense trying to hunt him down now. Nothing we got to ride could hope to catch that thoroughbred. So let's hope we've seen the last of the ornery cuss, whoever he was."

Munro laughed and said he hoped so, too.

CHAPTER FOUR

A man could see far and wide from his front window once he'd built his sod house atop a prairie rise. So Silas Dorman was standing in his open doorway on the afternoon of New Year's Day as Mingis Munro rode into his dooryard aboard a livery stable plug, leading a frisky black pony with Morgan lines and saddled with a black and silver Vadelia.

Munro had used some of his mustering-out money to replace his army greatcoat with a more sensible sheepskin. As he reined in, the older man in the doorway called out, "I know who you are. You're the young gent who gunned Blacky Dawson last night. What brings you all the way out here, son?"

Munro hadn't been invited to dismount, so he stayed put atop the old crowbait as he replied, "This other critter was left at the livery by the late Mister Dawson. The town law said he was mine now, if I wanted him."

Silas Dorman nodded and said, "That sounds reasonable. But if you come to me to sell him, you made a mistake. It's true I deal in horses, but I got more than I know what to do with, since the army remount service has been cutting back."

Munro said, "I didn't bring him to sell him, sir. He's your'n for the asking. I know he ain't no thoroughbred. But you can see he's part Morgan, and his teeth say he's no more'n three or four."

"You brung that horse all the way out here to give him away, free? What makes you so generous, son?"

Munro shrugged and said, "You lost a good horse last night. I didn't steal it. But you might not have lost it if the owner of this one hadn't started up with me. So I figure you have as good a claim to it as me. Do you want it or don't you?"

Dorman's weather-beaten face softened slightly as he said, "Tether 'em both and come on in so's we can talk about it over coffee and cake."

Munro nodded and dismounted to do so as the older man stared impassively from the doorway. When he'd finished, Dorman led him into a good-sized sitting room with a cottonwood fire burning briskly in as baronial a fireplace as one could manage with whitewashed sod.

As Munro removed his hat, his host showed him to a leather chesterfield near the fire and told him to take off his sheepskin while he was at it, explaining, "Cottonwood don't give off as much heat as it should. But it's still a lot colder outside and a far ride back to town with no winter chaps."

Dorman moved to a doorway and called out a girl's name. As he rejoined Munro on the chesterfield, a pretty young gal wearing blue-checked gingham and ash-blond hair came in to join them. As Munro leaped to his feet, his host said, "June, this is Mingis Munro. My daughter, June, Mingis. Could we manage some coffee and cake for our guest, honey?"

She said it would be her pleasure and went to fetch it as her father confided, "She's as sweet as her late mother and almost as pretty. Don't come courting. She ain't old enough."

Munro said, "I wasn't planning on hanging about that long, sir. I'd be leaving on the train this evening if they hadn't put me in for the reward money on that Dawson gent. They say there's some paperwork involved, and of course the money has to come all the way from Cheyenne."

Dorman nodded and said, "It usually takes at least a couple of weeks. Maybe more in this case. The man you gunned was quite a boy. He was wanted lots of places, and you stand to collect a considerable sum. No offense, son. But you just ain't my picture of a gun slick good enough to take a man of Blacky Dawson's breed."

Munro nodded and replied, "I ain't. It was a fluke."

The girl came back with refreshments on a tray. She put them on a low teak table between the chesterfield and the fire. Her father nodded, and she took a seat on a nearby stool to pour.

Dorman waited until they were working on the coffee and layer cake before he said, "You learned to shoot a gun somewhere, and you do seem to know which end of a horse the apples fall from. I don't recall seeing you around Medicine Wells before, son."

Munro began to bring them up to date on his recent past. June was staring at him big-eyed by the time he got to the part about losing a lung and his employment with the War Department as well.

"That wasn't fair. It wasn't your fault the Indians acted so mean!" she said.

Munro shrugged and said, "I ain't as sore as I was, now that I've had time to study on it, ma'am. Army life was sort of tiresome, even when we got to chase Mister Lo around.

With the Indian wars over, the army will be cutting back even more, and Lord knows when I'd ever get another stripe. Even as a buck sergeant I was only making about as much as a trail hand can demand these days."

Her father asked, "Do you think you're worth more than a trail hand, Mingis?"

Munro said, as bluntly, "I hope so. I need to get back in shape before I could ask for top-hand wages. But I wasn't bad with a throw rope when I joined up, and I've learned a lot more about horses since then."

Dorman swallowed the last of his coffee and said, "June, why don't you go out front and tell us what you think of the black pony tethered there?"

She looked surprised but did as she was told. As she stepped outside, her father told Munro, "I'll put it to you plain and simple. I raise horses. I don't need cowhands, and I got all the stable boys I need. I like your style. I know you can ride, and last night you proved how good you are with a gun. If you want a job, I can pay you a dollar a day and found to start with. More if you work out right."

"Doing what?" asked Munro.

Dorman said, "The country's filling up faster than the Indians can get off it. We've already had some cow stealing, and horses are worth more. It's only a question of time before we start losing stock, and you saw last night how enthusiastic the local law is about catching horse thieves. I need hands who take my property rights more serious."

"In other words, you want to hire my gun hand, not my roping skills or range savvy. Sir?"

Dorman shrugged and said, "Cowhands come a dime a dozen, and they're worth no more when hardcases raid stock the cowboys don't own and see no reason to risk their lives protecting. So, yeah, I need at least a few hardcases like you on my payroll."

The girl came back in, beaming, to say, "Oh, it's a sweet little pony, Father. Are you going to buy him?"

Dorman looked at Munro with a curious smile. Munro said, "He's a present, Miss June. Just who I give him to is up to your dad, here."

Dorman asked, "Do you want him, honey?"

The girl clapped her hands like a child and gushed, "Oh, ever so much! He's just beautiful, Father!"

The two men exchanged glances. Then Dorman said, "I reckon he's yours, then. Mingis, here, will be going to work for us as head wrangler. So he'll be able to give you some pointers on the difference between your regular mounts and a real cow pony."

She dimpled at Munro and told him she just couldn't thank him enough. Munro was beginning to see why her father felt so protective of her. She had to be somewhere between sixteen to twenty, but she acted more like a ten-year-old. He didn't know her well enough to decide whether she was retarded or oversheltered. It hardly seemed likely he'd ever find out. He got to his feet and said, "The horse is yours, Miss June. But I fear I won't be here to teach you to ride it. Just remember, a cow pony takes every signal you give it three times more serious than a regular riding horse, and you won't get into too much trouble."

Her father rose as well, with a frown, to say, "You won't get a better offer at any other spread in these parts, son."

Munro said, "I know. Like I said, I wasn't planning on staying up here in Wyoming. As soon as I get that reward money, I'll be on my way south."

"To do what? Start your own herd down Texas way?"

"The thought had occurred to me, sir. But some of that money has to be set aside for a pard of mine. So I reckon I'll play it by ear as I go. That sure was fine coffee and cake. I got to get back to town now. I hired that other brute by the hour."

They both walked him out front. June patted her new pony's muzzle and called it a darling as Munro untethered his stable nag. As he was about to mount up, Silas Dorman said, "I don't understand you at all, son. Didn't you just offer us that Morgan in order to butter me up for that job?"

Munro said, "Nope. When I want a job, I generally just ask for it. No offense, sir, but you sure have a suspicious nature. Ain't nobody never done you a favor just to be friendly?"

Dorman said, "Not hardly. But I'll be damned if I don't think you're just what you seem to be. You really don't want nothing from us, do you?"

Munro swung up into the saddle before he replied, "I told you. If you had anything I wanted, I'd ask. I was brung up to do what I thought was right, not to beat about the bush."

He tipped his hat brim to them and neck-reined his mount to ride off. He reined in again when Silas Dorman called out to him again. As Munro waited politely, the old horse breeder said, "I may have spoke too hasty before about my daughter, here, receiving visitors. If you're still in town when they hold the dance at the Grange hall next month, I've no objections if you ask her—that is, if she wants to ride in with you."

June blushed and gasped, "Father! Is that any way to talk?"

Munro didn't blame her. He said, "I doubt I'll still be here, sir. But if I am, you have my word I won't be asking any other lady hereabouts."

Then he rode off before he could get into any more trouble. He muttered, "That'll larn you to act Christian in Wyoming, you damn fool. Didn't them Crow teach you anything at all?"

CHAPTER FIVE

By the time Munro had spent eight nights in his dinky room at the Bull Head he was sincerely tired of Medicine Wells and wondering whether Kiowa Culhane had ever learned to read. For although Munro's "duel" with the notorious Blacky Dawson had been picked up by the papers far and wide, Culhane had not come back from wherever he'd gone aboard Silas Dorman's best horse.

Munro was hard pressed to figure why. By now Culhane surely knew he was in the clear and the papers had carried more about the considerable reward money than Munro felt comfortable about. He could see, and surely Culhane could see, that half of it, if not more, was Kiowa's simple due. Even if Culhane thought the man he'd saved in that saloon fight meant to hold out on him, he couldn't be afraid to face down an erstwhile "pard" who was that much slower on the draw. The mysterious modesty on the part of a gent who'd never shown any modesty before made Munro sort of tense.

But on January 9, 1879, something happened that made more folk in Wyoming Territory tense. A delegation of townsfolk caught up with Munro as he was supping in a beanery near the depot and told him he was wanted at the town hall on the double.

Munro bolted the last of his coffee and got to his feet, asking why. One of the worried-looking men explained, "We just got word by wire from Camp Robinson. Dull Knife has busted out again. He's headed this way with close to four hundred bloodthirsty Cheyenne!"

Munro asked what in thunder they expected him to do about it.

An older man said, "Tell *us* what to do, of course. You have to know more about fighting Indians than anyone else in these parts."

Munro didn't know whether to laugh or cuss. So he just went with them. The nearby town hall was crowded as they led him in by a side door and up onto a low platform as if they expected him to make a fool speech. Some in the crowd applauded as he stood there grinning sheepishly. He recognized a lot of faces that had insisted on buying him drinks in the saloon down the street. They were all sober and sort of ashen-faced this evening. He saw more than one woman in the crowd. Silas Dorman was near the back with Miss June. So Munro knew he had to watch his mouth, and it was hard to talk about Indian fighting without cussing.

He asked the big shots on the platform with him if they had any real figures on paper to work with. One handed him the All Points wire from the BIA. He scanned it, nodded, and held up a hand for silence.

He didn't get much. But as it was at least quiet enough to be heard now, he yelled, "Simmer down and listen up. To begin with, it's mighty doubtful them poor confused Indians will make her anywhere near this far. Even if they manage, these figures ain't all that alarming. We got enough men in this very room to lick 'em if they're really on the warpath, which I'm sure they ain't."

That got them all going again. Some sounded cheered by

his words, while others expressed considerable doubt. A sort of hard-eyed but handsome woman dressed more cow than ladylike in sheepskin and split riding skirts elbowed her way to the front to demand a more sensible explanation. She added, "I got myself, an old man, and a boy of fourteen to hold my spread, a good five miles out on the prairie. So, saying we ain't really talking four hundred warriors, what *are* we talking and how on earth are we supposed to hold 'em off when they get here?"

A cowhand in back of her laughed and said, "Just rope and drag them like you done that cow thief last summer, Miss Lizzy."

From the way some others laughed Munro suspected the gal had a rep that went with her mannish stance and firm jaw line. But she was still a gal. So he nodded down at her politely and said, "If you're forted good behind stout sod walls, with windows on all four sides, you ain't likely to get attacked direct. But you could lose some stock, and it might be a good notion to recruit at least one more gun hand for that fourth window."

She nodded grimly and announced loudly, "I'm willing to pay a dollar a day to any man here who can handle a Winchester and knows better than to get forward with a strong-willed widow woman."

There was no takers. She called out to a cowhand she seemed to know, and he said, "I'd sure like to, Miss Lizzy. But I got my own stock and provisions to look after."

Munro said, "Hold on, now. You're all starting to get more excited than you need to again. In the first place, Dull Knife is traveling with way less than four hundred. The BIA says they make it a hundred and thirty-four kids, a hundred and twelve women, and no more than eighty-nine men. They count anything from a mean-eyed ten-year-old to an old crippled-up Indian as a man. So we're more likely talking fifty-odd real fighters, stuck with dependents to drag along or carry, and, like I said, they ain't about to get this far. If they make it across the White River, they'll be doing better than they ought to."

Someone demanded, "What makes you so sure of that, sonny?"

Another snapped, "He ain't a sonny, he just got outten the army wearing three stripes as well as all his hair. So he has to know *something* about Indians."

Munro nodded and said, "I do. This ain't the time to give you all a lecture on the history of the Indian wars. So I'll just ask you to take my word on Dull Knife and Little Wolf. This wire from Camp Robinson don't say, but it's a safe bet Dull Knife's subchief, Little Wolf, is with him. They're kin. Neither one has much common sense, as recent events keep proving."

The older man who'd called him sonny shouted, "That ain't what the papers have been saying about Dull Knife since September. It looks to me as if he's been making the army look dumb as hell, no offense and sorry, ladies."

Munro said, "None taken. The army is more used to dealing with fighting chiefs with sensible goals in mind. Red Cloud was a grand tactician, and Sitting Bull understood strategy more than Indians are supposed to."

Someone shouted, "What about Gall and Crazy Horse?"

Munro nodded and said, "They had the leadership ability of, say, a good platoon commander, and Red Cloud knew how to position his forces. But I said this wasn't the time for a rehash of the Indian wars. They're over. All the really good leaders are dead or domesticated, tonight. Dull Knife was never more than a sort of company commander during the Big Scare. With nobody over him to tell him what to do, he's been dream-singing."

He saw that was over their heads. So he explained, "He's reverted to what they call the Shining Times, afore we come out here to teach 'em serious warfare, when the life of a

43

High Plains warrior was a sort of religious experience. He's been getting his tactical directions from his spirits. That's what they call their dreams or visions from a bottle, spirits."

The doubting Thomas, who now seemed to doubt Munro less, protested, "He may be drunk. He may be dreaming. But he's still been making saps out of everyone since September!"

Munro nodded and said, "It's hard to figure what a drunk or lunatic will do next. Nobody expected them to bust out of Fort Reno because it made no sense to bust out that late in the year. None of the other bands down in the Indian Nation did anything but line up for their rations with winter coming on, did they? As for Dull Knife's band making it even as far north as the Nebraska Sand Hills before they were rounded up again, that was because he led 'em so *pointless*. They went around easy targets for a band that was on the warpath. They forded rivers where the fording was tough. Lord knows what they've been eating, because they never went near such buffalo herds as are left. As for this latest bust-out, I'll allow they made the troops guarding 'em at Camp Robinson look dumb, until you study on it."

The gal called Miss Lizzy said, "They *must* have been dumb. They had to know they were guarding known hostiles."

Munro nodded but said, "It snowed last night. This wire says those Cheyenne busted out in the middle of a blizzard. This is the middle of winter, and, no offense, it gets mighty cold up in these parts anywhere betwixt September to May. The soldiers had unhorsed and disarmed Dull Knife's band, or at least they thought they had. The squaws always hide a few weapons under their skirts or sort of wrapped up with a papoose. So, all right, let's say they did bust out armed and dangerous, on foot, in the dead of winter. How were the

44

soldiers supposed to know Dull Knife's spirits had ordered him to act crazy as *that*?"

The man who'd called him sonny insisted, "The point is that they did, and to get to their old hunting grounds along the Powder River, they got to come right through us!"

There was a worried murmur of agreement. Munro waved a hand for silence and said, "It don't matter how homesick Dull Knife and his Cheyenne might be. They can't be within a hundred and fifty snow-covered miles from here, on foot, with few blankets and no lodges. I'll allow they're brave. Lord knows they have to be determined, but the poor brutes are just plain doomed. If the troops following their clear trail across snow don't catch up with 'em any minute, the wolf wind will."

Miss Lizzy asked, "What if you're wrong? I've been caught in a blizzard with no shelter, and I'm still here. This is Cheyenne country. They have to be more used to the wolf wind than any of *us* are."

Munro shrugged and said, "Even if it was high summer and they was all mounted up, there's no way they'd get a hundred and fifty miles in less than a week. Four days, tops. So I suggest you all go home and wait at least a few days afore you consider forting up."

"What about our stock?" she demanded, adding, "I can't hide even one longhorn under my kitchen table, you know."

Munro laughed at the mental picture and said, "This weather is sure to kill more stock than any Indians, even if the Indians get anywhere near 'em. You folk are all het up over nothing. Why don't you all go home in case it starts snowing again tonight."

One of the men who'd dragged him away from his supper said, "We were sort of counting on you to take charge of our defenses, Sergeant Munro."

Munro blinked, laughed, and said, "Shoot, I just told you there was nothing to worry about. I reckon I enjoy giving orders as much as the next man, but I'd be acting the fool if I tried to play general when there's no real emergency."

One of the older men who'd been in the saloon while Blacky Dawson was still spread out like a floor rug shouted, "I say we listen to the sergeant. He's a real fighting man, and he's used to giving orders. If he says he has no orders to give, that's good enough for me."

Someone else said, "Let's go over to the saloon and have a drink on it."

He didn't have to repeat his suggestion. The town hall began to clear out. Munro ducked out the side door lest they drag him along or lest Silas Dorman try to match him up with Miss June again. He didn't want to go to bed drunk tonight, and even if he wanted to spark June Dorman, he didn't have enough pocket jingle left to consider it. So far all that talk about reward money had just been talk, and he was trying to be careful with his mustering-out pittance.

As he crunched toward his hotel in the darkness, the widow woman called Miss Lizzy fell in step beside him, saying, "I wish I could buy your words of cheer, Sergeant. But to tell the truth, I'm still spooked."

He said, "Call me Mingis. I ain't a sergeant no more."

She said, "All right. You can call me Liz, then. I hate to be called Lizzy. What sort of name is Mingis, anyway? It sounds Indian. But you can't be a breed with such fair hair and hazel eyes."

He said, "I know there's Mingo Indians. But in my case Mingis is an old Scots name. I was named after a grandfather from the old country. It could have been worse. My other grandfather was named Dugal."

She chuckled and said, "My folk was Germans afore they was Texans. My married name is Stanhope. I think my late husband's kin come to Texas by way of England. He was killed a year ago come green up. We never had prairie dogs enough to worry about in Texas. So he was chasing a calf across a prairie dog town at a dead run when, next thing he knew, his pony's leg and his neck got busted one-two-three."

Munro said he was sorry to hear that and added he'd had some close calls with prairie dog holes.

She said, "So have I. You get to where you can spot 'em, though. I didn't follow you from that meeting to talk about the past. You said something about that fourth window. I've heard a lot about you since the other night you won that shoot-out. I know you ain't been paid for your trouble yet. I'm willing to pay a dollar a day and found, and, in all modesty, I ain't a bad cook."

He laughed incredulously and said, "That's the second such offer I've had, Miss Liz. I don't know why there's such a market for hired guns around here."

She said, "You ought to. You shot one just the other night. This country is thin-settled, and thin-settled country is dangerous, even when there ain't no Indians prowling about. I ain't asking you to hire on regular, Mingis. Just till we find out if you're right or wrong about them Cheyenne. I told you I got an old man and a boy out at my spread, in case you're worried about your virtue."

He laughed and said, "I ain't worried as *you* ought to be, no offense. You're a lot prettier than me."

She said, "I know what I look like. Do you want the job or don't you?"

He started to say no. Then he wondered why anyone would want to say a dumb thing like that. So he said, "I could use the free grub as well as the money. But I'd be robbing a woman alone if I took more than room and board for doing nothing. I'd be willing to ride out to your spread and ease your mind if I had anything to ride, Miss Liz."

She slapped him on the back and said, "There you go. I drove my buckboard in this evening to pick up provisions.

47

That's when I first heard about them fool Cheyenne busting loose again. It's down by the livery. I couldn't leave my team out in this cold."

He said in that case he'd check his duffle out of the hotel and join her there. Twenty minutes later, he had and they were driving out across the snow-covered prairie. It was a clear night. But the moon didn't give much warmth, and Munro was shivering some by the time they were halfway there. She clucked the team faster and told him, in that motherly way he hated to hear coming from pretty gals who didn't have a gray hair to call their own, that he should have picked up some winter chaps by now.

He said, "I've been told that afore, too. Woolly chaps ain't cheap, and I'd look silly in 'em once I got back to Texas."

She asked, "Why do you want to go back to Texas? I know you come from there. But so do I, and most of the stock grazes up here on the grass of Goodnight."

He said, "That sounds sort of poetical. I've never heard this old Cheyenne-Crow hunting ground called anything that nice."

"That's likely because you were gazing at it with army eyes. Captain Charlie Goodnight found the best grass on the High Plains when he found the grass around here. It ain't just that we get more rain this far north. There's something in the soil, or mayhap in the sort of shortgrass that grows up here, that puts twice the beef on a cow for half the grazing. It's good for growing bones, too. Both ponies and cows grow up faster on the grass of Goodnight."

He said grudgingly, "Well, Mister Lo did hunt a mess of big fat buffalo, on mighty fast ponies, in his Shining Times. But they was all critters created for such country, like that Professor Darwin would have it. Neither Texas folks nor Texas longhorns was ever created for Wyoming winters."

They'd just topped a rise, and as they got closer to the

dark mass in the draw beyond, he could see it was a clump of cows huddled with their rumps to the wind from the northwest. Liz Stanhope pointed her buggy whip that way and said, "Those longhorns are part of my Lazy S herd. There are more in the other draws all about. Down Mexico way, where we got 'em in the first place, longhorns grow more horn and hide than beef. They're a mighty tough breed some say the Moors brought to Spain from north Africa to begin with. They can thrive in desert country good as goats. But Captain Goodnight wasn't crazy when he brung the first herds of longhorn north, along his trail over to the west. Those cows are so used to getting by on wisps of cheat grass and desert scrub that they get downright overweight on the really nourishing range up here. You'd be surprised how much cold a cow can take with some fat under its hide. As for Texas folk, all of us but the Mexicans and Indians seem to have surnames from the north of Europe. We may be used to warmer winters ourselves, but our ancestors lived through an ice age that had to be as bad as a Wyoming winter, right?"

He huddled deeper into the collar of his sheepskin as he said, "If you say so. They say my clan come from the north of Scotland, and I know I've lived through three winters up this way. But so far I ain't started to *enjoy* 'em much."

She laughed and said, "Nobody with a lick of sense could enjoy a Wyoming winter. But the summers more than make up for 'em, if you're really interested in raising stock. My late husband and me had much the same argument the first time in my life I saw snow and heard the wolf wind howling outside our soddy. But he was right to drive our modest herd up the Goodnight Trail as soon as we heard the Indians had been scattered after Little Big Horn. The scare was still on. So we got other cows cheap as we moved in a mite early. Had not it been for that infernal prairie dog town. . . . But never mind. That light ahead is my place."

Munro was sincerely hoping it was, as they seemed to be taking forever to reach the slowly growing candle beam. As they drove over a cattle guard into her dooryard, he could see the candle was lit in a small window by the front door, under a low flat overhang. The roof was covered with snow. He figured it had to be sod. Shingle roofs needed to slope more to keep the meltwater out.

As Liz reined in, the door popped open and a skinny kid ran out with a shotgun. He lowered the muzzle when he saw who he'd just heard coming. He bawled, "Judas Priest, Miss Liz. I feared you'd been scalped by now! A rider from the K Slash J was by just a few minutes ago to warn you the Cheyenne has riz again!"

She said, "I know. Mingis, this is Bob Westwood, our wrangler. Mister Munro will be staying with us until the army does something about those Indians, Bob. Is Uncle Jim still up?"

The kid said, "Not hardly. He found that bottle you hid under the dry sink, Miss Liz. I put him in his bunk to sleep it off."

She sighed and said, "My fault, I guess. Would you put the team away, oated and rubbed good, Bob? I'll show our guest where he can but his possibles."

Munro remembered his manners in time to leap out first to help her down from the rig. She looked surprised but not displeased. She led him inside. The lodgepole-raftered ceiling was lower than he'd have made it, but the soddy made up for that by being spacious, with low doorways leading off mysteriously. She led him through one, into a fair-sized room with one small window. There were boxes and barrels along the sod walls but nothing that looked like a bed. She told him he could drop his duffle anywhere and added, "I'll have Bob break out a folding cot for you as

50

soon as he comes in from bedding down the team. We got a lot of army surplus this fall at a bargain. Do you think they mean to close that post down entire, Mingis?"

He followed her back out as he told her, "I don't know. They sure have been cutting expenses since President Hayes took over back east. He was elected on a promise to balance the budget, and closing down Indian fighting posts makes sense now that there's so few Indians left to fight."

She led him into what seemed an all-purpose kitchen, dining and sitting room and sat him at a trestle table as she peeled out of her own sheepskin, saying, "I'll start some coffee for us. I did have almost a full pint of bourbon. But you heard Bob say what happened."

He nodded and asked, "Are the two of 'em kin to you or what, Miss Liz?"

She turned to her stove and shoved another stick in the fire box as she said, "I'd hate to think I was really related to Uncle Jim. He was distant kin to my late husband. He and some others hired on to help us drive our herd up the Goodnight Trail. The others quit once we paid 'em off, of course. Uncle Jim just sort of stayed on. My husband fired him, more than once. But the poor old cuss just moped about like an old lost dog, and, well, I reckon I'm just weak-willed, and if those Indians do show up, he may wind up earning his keep after all. He's not really bad. He's just sort of old and useless."

"What about the kid outside, Miss Liz?"

She shrugged and said, "He earns his keep. I hire extra hands at day wages during roundups and market drives. But even when it's slow out here, there's more work than a woman alone can handle. I've taught him to wrangle, and he's willing to try any chores I give him. He's stronger now than when we found him. He may turned out a fair cowhand in time."

51

As she set water on to boil, he asked just what she meant by "finding" the kid.

She said, "He run off from some orphan asylum back east, and they throwed him off a freight car in the Medicine Wells yards, with a warning to start walking and not come back. The poor fool kid was eight miles out on the prairie, hunkered in the grass by the trail and trying not to cry, when I come by on my bronc to ask him what on earth he was doing out there."

She flared a mite as she added, "I reckon you think I'm a natural fool, don't you?"

He said, "No, ma'am. I think you must be a kind Christian woman, even if you are sort of impulsive. The thing I like best is that you call him Bob instead of Bobby. I used to be fourteen, and I know what it feels like to be treated like a child when you're trying so hard to act like a man. Fourteen is a disgusting age to be, even when you ain't an orphan."

She smiled down at him and said, "No offense, Mingis, but I can't help suspecting your teenaged troubles were more recent than mine. How old do I look to you?"

He regarded her thoughtfully before he answered. Now that she was out of her shapeless sheepskin, he could see she was built sort of boyish and athletic for a gal, albeit no man was likely call her exactly skinny, and certainly not flat-chested. Her skin was smoother and whiter near the cuffs and neck V of her man's work shirt. Her face was more cured by wind and sun than by time's crueler teeth. She wore her dark hair down, like an Indian gal, but it was softer and wavier, and the ends were streaked lighter by the sun's bleaching than they'd started out. He said, "Well, since you had to ask, I'd say you could be anywheres between a well-preserved thirty-year-old to a mighty tough maid of sixteen."

She laughed like hell and said, "You're not a soldier. You're a trained diplomat. How old are you, Mingis?"

He said, "Old enough to know better and young enough to try. I mean to vote for President Hayes if he runs again, if that's what you mean."

He was saved from further embarrassment by the wrangler, Bob, coming in just then. The kid was shivering and blowing on his hands as he sat down at the table and said, "Judas Priest, it's getting cold out there. We could be in for a real blue norther by sunup."

Liz said, "Next time you run outside, put your fool coat on. The wind is too westerly for a blue norther, Bob. Ain't that right Mingis?"

Munro said, "A real blue norther generally comes from north-northeast, and not every winter, praise the Lord. But as long as we're on the subject of running outdoors at night, would you hold still for some well-meant advice on the subject?"

The boy looked blank. Liz said, "He's an old Indian fighter, Bob."

Bob asked what else he'd done wrong.

Munro said, "Never run out into the dark with the light behind you to investigate a noise, Bob. If it's a critter you heard, it'll be long gone by the time your eyes adjust to the dark. If it's something worse, you'll likely wind up shot. It's best to douse the light inside and ease over to a window not too near the door for a look-see. Anyone out there will generally come on in to knock polite or scamper off when they see by the way you've put out your lights that you're onto them."

The kid said, "Gosh. That makes so much sense, as soon as you study on it. You must think I'm awful green, huh?"

Munro shook his head and said, "Nobody ever starts out an old-timer, and we'll all still be green about something till the day we die. It's when a man thinks he knows all about everything that he's really green, Bob. If ever you find yourself feeling dead certain about anything that could possibly hurt you, back off and try to remember this conversation.''

Liz put cups and saucers for the three of them on the table as she told the boy, "Pay attention to him, Bob. He'd the one I told you about. The one who shot it out with Blacky Dawson last week."

The kid stared open-mouthed at Munro and said, "You ain't just greening me, are you?"

Munro sighed and said, "I wish I was. That was a case of a man feeling too smart for his own good, too. The next time I see a hardcase with that look on his face I'll know better. But I'd fought Sioux, Cheyenne, and Arapaho, and I still didn't recognize Mister Death staring me right in the face until it was almost too late."

"You must be quick as lightning on the draw," the kid said in a tone full of hero worship. Munro looked away and didn't answer. It made him feel low to take credit for a marvel he'd been credited with by mistake. It would have been even worse to tell them Kiowa Culhane had saved his fool neck and then stolen the horse Silas Dorman was still looking for.

Liz coffeed and grubbed them with a bedtime snack of scrambled eggs and apple pie. None of them knew why her apple pie was so good, even though she admitted to German ancestry. For by that winter apple pie had been established as the all-American pie, though the recipe handed down from her great-grandmother was the national dessert of Old Franconia. Munro just thought it tasted swell and didn't argue when she pressed seconds on him. Then she told Bob to break out that army cot and put it together for Munro in the spare room, taking the edge off what might have been a perfect evening, even if she was a mite old for him.

CHAPTER SIX

The next day dawned bright and sunny. The wind had died, and the thin, dry air, while hardly balmy, at least felt like that of a nippy spring day despite the snow on the ground all around. Munro felt dumb pretending to guard the spread from Indians he'd told them all not to worry about. So he followed young Bob out to tend to the morning chores. The kid seemed sort of possessive about the nine ponies in the sod stable. So as Bob watered and oated them, Munro found a dung fork and proceeded to muck out the stable. It was more than a mite overdue. It had always been more fun to feed and pet ponies than to clean up after them.

He was forking manure-soaked straw bedding into a wheelbarrow in the open doorway when a surly male voice asked him who the hell he was and what the hell he thought he was doing.

He looked up at the dirty old man in gray beard and blue bib overalls to say, "My name would be Mingis Munro. I can see why you'd be confused about what I'm doing, Uncle Jim. For this stable ain't been mucked for some time, and Miss Liz tells me this spread is only a couple of years old."

The old man asked, "How did you know my name, damn it? I ain't never met up with you before."

The boy, Bob, came out from the stalls to call out, "Don't mess with him, you old fool. He's the one as beat Blacky Dawson to the draw the other night."

The old man blanched. Munro frowned at the boy and said, "That's no way to talk to your elders, Bob. A man riding ramrod for a spread has a right to know what a stranger's doing near the livestock. You just go on about your chores and make sure you water afore you oat, instead of the other way around."

Bob said, "Shoot. I know better than to bloat a pony," and left them alone to sort it out. As Munro had hoped, his implied respect had more than mollified the older man. Uncle Jim held out a dirty hand, and, as long as he was mucking horse manure in any case, Munro took it so they could shake friendly.

Uncle Jim said, "I can tell from the way you talk you're a Texan as well as a gent. I knowed some Munro folk years ago. On the Brazos it was. They branded A Slash M."

Munro said, "That would be my own Uncle Angus, sir. I'm sorry to say he died in the war. His spread was sold for back taxes during the Reconstruction."

The old man sighed and said, "There's been times I wished I'd fallen for the Cause. They said I was too old to ride for Texas agin' the blue bellies, even then. I reckon you'd have been too young for the war, right?"

"Yes, sir. Too young for that one. I just finished a hitch sort of calming down Mister Lo."

Uncle Jim frowned thoughtfully, then decided, "Well, I reckon a fighting Texan with no chance to wear butternut has the right to fight in blue as long as it's just agin' Injuns.

56

Blacky Dawson was a damnyankee, you know. He should have known better than to mess with us Texans, even if he was a hired gun."

Munro almost let that go. Then he said, "That's the second time I've heard Dawson called a hired gun. It was my understanding he was more like an outlaw."

Uncle Jim said, "That, too. You must have noticed as you was killing him that he was crazy-mean. But it was well knowed he could be hired for assassination pure and simple. You know how it works, don't you, son? Say you don't like someone, only you aint ready to go up agin' him yourself, for whatever reason. So you pay a gent like Dawson to just pick a fight with him. They say Dawson was good at picking fights."

Munro frowned thoughtfully as he replied, "That was said true enough. But hold on. I can't think of a soul, aside from mayhaps some few Indians, who'd hire anyone to pick a fight with me, Uncle Jim."

The old man said, "Well, it could have been just for practice. Or he might have had a fight with someone else in mind and you just sort of got in the way."

Munro thought back to those bewildering, noisy moments in the saloon and said, "I hadn't studied on that. Seeing you know Texas and Texans so well, Uncle Jim, have you ever heard of a gent called Culhane?"

"Kiowa Culhane? The kid from the Staked Plains country who made such a name for hisself slaughtering Kiowa in and out of season? Sure. They say when he signed up for the buffalo war he had his rifle strap all dingle-dangle with Indian scalps. Last I heard, he'd been killed at Little Big Horn with Custer."

Munro shook his head and said, "Not hardly. He was there, but with Benteen's command. I know some think the whole Seventh Cav was wiped out there. But it was only a third of the outfit. The confusion is no doubt caused by the fact Custer was with the third they run over. Culhane was with the ones who fought their way out, and until recently I was in his new outfit with him."

The old man seemed neither surprised nor dismayed. He said, "Well, that just goes to show how hard it is to kill a Texan. Do we have some reason to be talking about that murderous young cuss, even if he is from down home, son?"

They didn't unless Munro wanted to tell more about Culhane than Culhane might want bruited about. So he said, "I just saw Kiowa the night Dawson acted so wild. Wondered if they might not know each other, is all."

The old man said he had no idea, added he was cold, and headed back to the house. As Munro continued to muck, he went over the otherwise senseless shoot-out in his head yet another time and remembered that Kiowa had said he had no idea who the hard-eyed cuss was. Munro sighed, heaved another forkful into the wheelbarrow, and muttered, "I may never get to the bottom of this blasted mess."

"Are you talking to yourself?" asked Liz Stanhope as he dug down for some more muck. He stood up to lean on the fork handle with a sheepish grin as he replied, "I didn't see you sneaking up on me. Everybody talks to themselves. Don't you?"

She laughed and said, "I can see a lady has no secrets from you. Why on earth are you mucking like a stable hand? I have my own help to do that, Mingis."

He saw she was dressed warmly but lighter than the day before and had a riding quirt hanging from her right wrist. He said, "I just mentioned the condition of your stable bedding to your help. Your ponies are going to wind up with hoof rot unless someone spreads clean straw for 'em to stand on."

She said, "Oh. I thought you might like to join me as I ride out for a look at my herd. I don't think that last snowfall could have taken any. But I like to be sure."

He leaned the fork aside and said, "I'd like that, if you have a spare saddle. I can see you have enough of a remuda to outfit guests for riding."

She led him into the tack room and pointed out a double-rig roping saddle, saying, "That's not the one my husband was riding when he died, in case you're superstitious. I got rid of it. I reckon I'm superstitious, too."

She started to pick up a smaller, center-fire saddle, saying it was hers. Munro tried to take it from her. She resisted and told him, "You saddle your pony, and I'll saddle mine. That way neither of us will feel as silly if we're spilled by a loose cinch."

He said that sounded fair, picked up the double-rig, and they went out to the stalls to choose and saddle up. Or, that is, she told him a big blue gelding was his to ride without asking how he felt about the brute.

She chose a smaller and prettier buckskin mare. He wasn't too surprised she'd done the picking. He was beginning to see that she was a good old gal but sort of sure of things for a woman. They bridled and saddled and led the ponies outside to mount up. As he raised his left arm to haul himself aboard with a fistful of rein and mane, he was suddenly aware of all the manure he'd just forked. It didn't hurt. His left side just felt more *there* than he was used to. He realized this would be the first time he'd ridden since that arrow had dismounted him so unexpectedly.

But once he was in the saddle it felt right again. Liz took the lead. Her buckskin was frisky and danced nervously over the cattle guard when they came to it. The blue he was on just picked its way through the five logs laid like railroad ties as it wasn't at all surprised to be smarter or at least more sure-footed than any old cow.

Once they were out on the wagon trace, Liz let out a joyous whoop, gave her mount a lick with her quirt, and they were off to the north at a good lope.

Munro had neither quirt nor spurs to work with. So he could only heel the big blue and hope it wouldn't make him look like a total sissy.

It didn't. It obeyed his heels as if they'd been big old Mex rowels and lit out after the gal and her show-off pony in a no-nonsense manner. It loped leading with its off-forehoof, as a well-trained roping pony was supposed to. Munro experimented with neck-reining, and the big blue was immediately off the wagon trace and loping across the snow due west, as if it thought it was a grand notion to chase invisible whatevers. Munro laughed, swung it back the other way, and was still chuckling when they caught up with Liz, who'd slowed to walk her mount up a rise. She smiled and said, "I figured you two would get along. He's a mite big for me to handle once he's chasing a calf serious. As you can see by my saddle, I'm a dally roper. Old Blue was broke in tie-down, and he stops on a dime and digs in the second you throw."

Munro patted the big brute's neck and said, "I like him. You wasn't being as dispolite as I thought back there. But how come you own a mount you don't fancy riding?"

She said, "I bought him cheap. It was a distress sale. A trail herder had a bad run at cards in town and needed traveling money to get home more than he needed most of his remuda. He auctioned off all but his Sunday pony. I bid on that one when I saw a chance to pick up a good cow pony cheap. I reckon some of the others were smarter than me in the end. Like I said, there are times he needs a stronger hand than mine to handle him. You want him?"

Munro blinked in surprise and said, "I might, if I meant to stay in these parts. What are you asking for him?"

"I paid fifteen bucks. He's worth more. You can have him for ten, and if you're short of cash, you can owe me."

It was a hell of a bargain, and they both knew it. He said, "I'll have to study on it. Like I said, I mean to head back to Texas as soon as I pick up that bounty money, and I doubt he could ride for half fare, even if he does look less than twelve."

"You'll still need something to ride until you have to leave, unless you spend *all* your time in saloons," she pointed out as they started out again at a conversational walk.

He knew that was true. The livery in town charged outrageous fees for the hire of pure crowbait. But he liked to take time to make his mind up, when he had the chance. So he said, "I see you got less than five acres fenced in back there. What do you really hold, the usual quarter-section homestead claim?"

She shook her head and said, "Full section. We're still on it. It takes five years and a lot of pesky paperwork to prove a homestead, and the land office is willing to sell this reclaimed Indian land for two bucks an acre, clear title."

He counted in his head, whistled softly, and said, "Well, if you got a square mile for less than thirteen hundred dollars, I can't say you got robbed."

She said, "It's sure to go up in price as more settlers move in. This is the time to grab your share of the grass of Goodnight, Mingis. If you're right about the Indian wars being over, this territory will attract stockmen like honey draws flies. For the price of beef is rising, and any fool who can tell a cow from a jackrabbit can make money at the game now."

As they topped the rise, she pointed down at a dozen head

61

of fat and sassy steers pawing at the deeper snow in the draw ahead and said, "Speaking of jackrabbits, them's mine, and as you can see, a little snow don't bother them. They like the grass in the bottom of draws best. It takes longer to summer-brown, and the stems stay tasty, even dried out. Lots of starch in the grass Captain Goodnight found for us."

Munro said, "That's likely why Mister Lo and his buffalo held out longer up this way. But them longhorn ain't buffalo. So what happens if you get a really bad blue norther up here on this north range, Miss Liz?"

She shrugged and said, "We lose some stock. Just like you do on the balmy Texas plains when there's a drought. If grazing stock held no risk at all, nobody would plant corn or teach school. A killing dry spell south of the Arkansas comes more often than a killing winter up this way. So it more than evens out."

They rode on. She spotted more cows farther out and said they were hers, save for one with shorter horns and another brand. "I figured we had to be on open range by now. What's the story on grazing fees?" Munro asked.

She said, "They're supposed to be ten cents a head. So far, nobody's ever seen fit to collect fees for Uncle Sam's grass in these parts, though."

He nodded and said, "It'd barely pay. How do you manage the roundup? Gather privately, or consolidated?"

She said, "Consolidated. Saves work for everyone, and so far none of the local outfits have enough riders or even cows to play dirty. We all do our own spring branding, of course. But at market time we just get together to organize a collective roundup, work together to drive the consolidated herd to the railroad, and figure who owns what as the buyers bid on 'em."

He said, "That's the way we used to do her on the

Brazos, when it was less crowded and we all knowed each other better. If it wasn't for that snow all about, this country would remind me of the way Texas was when I was little."

She nodded and said, "That's how come so many Texas folks are moving up this way. We all like Texas better when we was little. Between the Reconstruction and all them big-money cattle outfits crowding in, raising stock down there has become big business. Up here is where the future lies for getting started. All you really need is a patch of land, at least one fertile cow, and a little time to pass."

"Don't you need a heap of luck as well?"

"Hell, you need luck to make it at anything. I told you about my late husband's luck with prairie dogs. But all in all, I've seen more good fortune than bad since we left a mighty dusty stretch of west Texas. I got my brand on close to four hundred head now, and at the rate they're increasing, I'll soon have to hire a full-time crew."

He thought and decided, "The spring calving ought to give you at least another dozen or so. I take it you'll be saving all your she-calves for your herd bull?"

She didn't fluster up as some gals might have when the topic of breeding came up. She simply said, "I don't have enough brood cows to pay for keeping any he-brutes yet. But I have been sort of keeping the she-males and selling off the ones birthed with balls as steer meat. I figure a girl-cow can get in the family way on her own just grazing about on open range unchaperoned. For how often might a stray bull wearing someone else's brand worry about the brand of a passionate stranger?"

He looked away as he opined, "Well, it ain't as if it's important to keep track of bloodlines in a scrub herd. But when and if I get my own herd, I mean to buy at least one good bull and see if I can't breed 'em up a mite."

She asked, "To what? There's no way to improve the longhorn as it comes natural."

He shrugged and replied, "That depends on whether one wants to raise beef or eat it. With this depression winding down, the housewives back east are sure to get more picky as they get used to serving steak and potatoes more regular. I like my own beef lean, and I ain't too lazy to chew. But more fussy dudes are sure to pay more for more tender beef. I figure a good white-face or Durham bull might breed up a starting herd of longhorns to more tender beef without taking all the range toughness out of 'em."

She started to object. But she was fair-minded as well as cow-savvy. So she said, "White-faces might make it through the winters out here. I wouldn't bet on any fancier eastern beef breeds, though. I can see why you feel Texas-bound. But how on earth do you figure to get started down there now, unless you have real cash or mayhaps help from your folk?"

He said, "I've been studying on that, too. I don't have no folk, now."

She said, "Oh, I'm sorry. What took 'em so young, the Yellow Jack or Comanche?"

He looked away and said, "Neither. I never said they was *dead*." Then he said, "Come on, let's lope, I'm getting chilled just moping about out here."

He heeled the big blue into a run. She followed. But as they tore down a rise at a dead run, she called out, "Not so fast with snow on the ground, damn it."

He ignored her warning until he felt his mount catch a hoof on something under the crust, skip, and then recover before he reined in. As she fell in beside him, calling him a fool, he said, "When you're right, you're right. I don't know what made me do that."

She said, "I do. But if you don't want to talk about

family matters, I won't press you. It was my fault for bringing private hurts up in the first place."

He said, "I ain't ashamed of my folk. I understand the way it was. Now that I'm growed up, leastways. I just don't like to talk about 'em no more. I ran like that because, like I said, it's too cold for just walking out here."

She said, "Let's head back, then. I can see that snowfall didn't hurt any stock, and you do look sort of froze. Is it that war wound, do you think?"

He waited until they'd swung around and were stirrup to stirrup again before he said, "I don't know. I feel all right most of the time. I feel better than I expected to this soon, as a matter of fact. But I suspect I might not be as strong as I was before, and while it don't hurt to breathe, I seem to *feel* my breathing more. I sure hope that passes before I have to do any real work."

She said she was sure it would and added, "You're already a lot stronger than me, and I feel fine the way I am. You don't rope left-handed, do you?"

He said, "Of course not. Even if I was a lefty, I'd have to rope right-handed. Cow ponies ain't trained to come in from the off side."

She said, "There you go. Your left hand seems to neck-rein pretty good already. Come green up you ought to be fit to rope and tie as good as ever."

They rode back a good quarter mile in silence. He found her company enjoyable whether they jawed or not. She seemed a good old gal. It was too bad she was older than him, and that June Dorman had to act so young. The only other gal he knew in these parts was Miss Trixie at the saloon, and the notion of sparking Miss Trixie was just awful.

It might not have happened had not Liz Stanhope seemed

65

so relaxed and undemanding. But he suddenly found himself blurting, "My folks got divorced."

She didn't look shocked. She just nodded and said, "Well, no doubt they felt they had a sensible reason, Mingis."

He said, "I wasn't there. It happened right after I joined the army. I suspect one of the reasons I joined up was to get away from the way they was tugging on me. First my mom would get me aside to tell me how bad he was, and then he'd try to get me to agree to his side."

"Whose side were you on the most?" she asked calmly.

He said, "Neither. I could see how both felt the justice of their position. They married young. Too young. They never should have married one another. But they did."

Liz seemed to be speaking partly to herself as she said, "I married young, too. But a gal who's anxious to get away from a strict home has to take the bad with the good. I'm sorry your mother was such a poor sport about the plain and simple fact that men and women both deserve something better than one another."

He said, "That's what I tried to tell 'em both. They'd made a deal. I figure a deal's a deal, don't you?"

She said, "Well, I can't say I ever considered divorce, even when I was sore at my man. It was easier to make up. More fun, too, come to study on it. We never had any kids afore he got killed young. So at least we got to fight fair, out in the open. It must have been rough on you, growing up."

He said, "I spent a lot of time over to friends and relations, learning to ride and work cows. I was on my own once I finished grade school and could hold a full-time job. So towards the end they could only corner me now and again, on holidays at home and such. You've no idea how a Thanksgiving turkey tastes when it's served by a weepy-eyed woman and the man who carves it ain't talking to her at all."

She said, "If a man did that to me, he'd get to cook his own infernal bird. But I can see why you joined the army as soon as you could."

He nodded and said, "It gave them the chance to end their big mistake, formal. They both had to leave town afterwards, of course. I don't recall anyone in our part of Texas getting no divorce. They must have been mad as hell at each other."

Liz said, "*I'd* have to be. Like you said, a deal is a deal as long as a man don't hurt you serious or bring home a dose of you-know."

He said, "My dad never hit her, and he wasn't a man for parlor houses, neither. Sometimes I think they'd have fought less if he *had* fooled around with other women."

"Oh? Was she denying him his marital rights?"

"Good Gawd, woman, is that any question to ask a man about his own mother? How in thunder would I be in any position to know?"

She said she was sorry for asking.

He said, "I do know she was bossy and sickly at the same time. I don't know what ailed her. But she sure spent a lot of time feeling poorly, and of course that meant she needed lots of help with the household chores, and, well, come to study on it, they did have separated rooms towards the end. Like I said, I can see better now how living with a gal like her might vex a big strong gent like my dad. He was only in his forties last time I saw him. He'd given up stock raising for a desk job with the railroad. But I doubt he ever learned to enjoy housework much. I know *I* never did. Mom was a sort of fussy housekeeper, and she lay on a sofa directing the way it should be done."

Liz shook her head and said, "He must have been a saint

unless he beat her when you weren't looking. I've met gals like that, and you're right, they never should get married. But somehow they always do. You men can be such fools about soft little things who look so pretty and helpless, until after the honeymoon."

He nodded grimly and said, "I figure I'll take more time than my dad did to get hitched. For one thing, a man has more choice in the matter if he waits until he's established, with something to offer a gal more substantial than candy, books, and flowers."

She shot him a little smile and told him he was no doubt very wise, adding, "You'll be beating them off with a club if you collect that reward money before the Grange dance next month."

He grimaced and said, "Oh, Lord, that settles it about Texas, then. I just remembered I sort of promised to take Silas Dorman's daughter to that dance if I'm still in these parts, no offense."

She said, "None taken. I wasn't planning on going. Us widow women are supposed to chaperone and serve the refreshments, and I'd rather dig post holes. I've seen June Dorman in town. She's a right pretty little thing, and not spoken for, I hear. She's an only child. So her father's out to match her with what you would call an established gent, knowing someday she'll own about the biggest spread in these parts."

He said, "Do tell? That's funny. I thought he just raised horses. You can't turn horses loose on open range."

She said, "I told you land was still cheap up here. Old Silas came to these parts well off and did even better with the army remount service during the Indian war. You could do a lot worse than June Dorman, Mingis. She's not only young and pretty, she's an heiress."

He sighed and said, "I mean to make my own fortune,

not marry up with it. You're right about her looks, and I know she bakes a fine cake. But I dunno, she strikes me more like a pretty china-headed doll than a real flesh and blood gal."

Then he laughed and said, "Lord have mercy, listen to me talking to you as if we was two old pals jawing about women instead of, well, a man and a woman!"

She nodded and said, "I want us to be pals, Mingis. I haven't had many men to talk to since I found myself alone, and none at all I could talk to so, well, free and easy-like. The few gents interested in sparking even a young widow woman tend to push the conversation to mushiness, or they act so shy there's no conversation at all. I got to watch what I say to young Bob or old Uncle Jim, lest Bob blush or Uncle Jim get disgusting. But with you, I can just let the words float out any way I feel like. I'm glad you felt you could trust me with your family scandal. For it means you feel the same way about talking to me. So tell me something, old pal, are you getting any in town or ain't you?"

He laughed, ears burning, and said, "Not hardly. Are you offering, or just curious?"

She said, "I ain't sure. We better change the subject."

He frowned and said, "You brung it up."

She said, "I know. It was dumb. Since we've agreed to be pals, I'm going to tell you one more thing I could only tell a real pal, and then, like I said, we'd best drop it for now."

He agreed, and she said, "It made me jealous, just now, when you said you might have to take June Dorman to the Grange dance. Wait, don't cut in. I know it was dumb. It surprised *me*, too. I hadn't been thinking about you that way, or at least I didn't think I was, until you painted me a picture of that pretty June Dorman in your arms, even doing no more than dancing. I caught myself about to say something spiteful. I didn't, because that wouldn't have been fair. She is pretty, and as far as I know, she's nice. Now, I want you to promise me that if you ever even kiss her, you won't tell me about it, hear?"

He nodded soberly and said, "That's easily done. I don't ever expect to. I wish you hadn't told me you felt jealous. I liked it better when, like I said, we was just talking about women like regular old pals."

She said, "I thought I did, too. I just learned something about myself I'm a mite ashamed of. I seem to have more natural feelings than I thought I did."

"Good Lord, about me, Miss Liz?"

"I'm not sure. Maybe just men in general. I've been alone a spell. Mayhap I'm just turning into a dirty old lady. But I don't want to get dirty with a man who's Texas-bound. So now that we have all the cards on the table, what say we just get up from the game with nobody the winner or loser."

He agreed that was more than fair and changed the subject to the way beef was marketed at the one railhead they had to drive it to.

She was explaining that while the railroad had a monopoly on freight charges, the buyers bidding on the beef were in hot competition and thus tended to keep the prices fair, when they both spotted another rider coming their way. She said, "Looks like Hank Mason off the Double Diamond. Wonder where he's headed in such a hurry."

As the woolly-chapped cowhand reined in with them, they found out. Mason said, "I just stopped by your spread with the news, Miss Liz. Your boy told me I might find you out this way, and seeing it wasn't too far out of my way home. . . ."

"This is Mingis Munro, Hank. He's a good old boy. What's up?"

"It's those Indians; more like down. The army caught up with Dull Knife's band just this side of the White River and spread at least fifty of 'em onto the snow like jam on bread. They're herding the survivors back to Camp Robinson about as fast as a Cheyenne can walk on frostbit feet, carrying a kid."

Mason shot a closer look at Munro and asked, "Say, ain't you the army gent as spoke about Dull Knife in town last evening?"

Munro nodded modestly, and the cowhand said, "You was right on the money about the White River. They never got within a hundred and fifty miles of here, like you said, and I for one mean to listen to you sharp the next time you opine on such matters!"

Mason filled them in on a few more grim details and then rode on to spread the joyous news. Liz waited until her spread was in sight again before she said, "Well, so much for my female notions about ferocious Cheyenne scalping us all in our nightgowns. Do you have anything more important to worry about in town or would you like to stay over, tonight at least?"

He said, "I'd best not. I'll take you up on the deal about this pony, provided you'll let me owe you a fairer price."

She said, "I named my price, and the saddle and bridle come with. How come you're in such an all-fired hurry to go, though, if it ain't June Dorman?"

He said, "It's not her or any other gal. I've been studying on that shoot-out I had in town, and the more I think on it, the more it seems to me I could be mixing you and your'n up in my own private trouble."

He told her his suspicions about Blacky Dawson being a hired gun.

She said, "But nobody hereabouts has been feuding, and

even if someone was, how could they have known you were coming in time to send for any hired gun?"

He said, "You got me there. But why take any chance at all with the safety of a pal like you? I'll be just as safe, and I'll know you-all are safe for sure, if I just hole up at my hotel again, see?"

She didn't seem to want him to. But his mind was made up, and it wasn't until they'd ridden in and he'd brought out his duffel that she threw her hat on the ground and kicked it.

He asked how come as he lashed the duffel to the saddle skirts of the big blue.

She said, "It's my hat, ain't it?"

He nodded and stepped around his mount to her side as he held out his hand and said, "I'll send the money out here when I get it, if I ain't got time to come myself, pal."

She said she wasn't sure she wanted to be his pal no more and headed for the stable, dragging her buckskin behind her, fast.

He shrugged, mounted up, and headed for town as he muttered to the big blue, "If I live to be a hundred, I'll just never understand womenkind. Whatever did I do or say to vex her so? I *told* her this was in her best interest. Why in thunder would she want me to spend another night out here, any damn ways?"

CHAPTER SEVEN

The railroad sent its bounty on Blacky Dawson at the end of the week. They only thought he was worth five hundred dollars to them, dead. But Wells Fargo, the Pinkertons, and First National of Wyoming had yet to be heard from.

The money order arrived a little after noon. So Munro took it to the Drover's Trust to cash and start a savings account. They seemed to know him at the bank and treated him like he was important even before he told them what he wanted. A chubby gent in a checked suit took Munro back to a private office and offered him a fine seat near his rolltop desk. He said there was no trouble about identification and that they'd be proud to give him the cash once he put his John Hancock on the back of the paper. When Munro said he only wanted a hundred of it and meant to bank the rest, he thought the banker was about to jump in his lap and lick his face. But he just got out a bankbook and proceeded to print Munro's name in it, neat as a sign painter might have. He wrote "Four hundred dollars" on the lined first page and said, "You can pick up your hundred at the window out front, sir. Is there anything else we can do for you?"

Munro said, "Yep. I should have spoke up sooner. But I want that to be a joint account. At least half the money belongs to an old army buddy of mine."

The banker said that would be no problem. But it turned out that it was. He asked when the joint depositer would be by to leave a signature on file with them.

Munro frowned and said, "To tell the truth, I ain't sure he can read and write. Can't I just sign for him?"

The banker looked prim and said, "I'm afraid not, sir. We know who you are. We couldn't just hand over money to a total stranger if we didn't even know what his signature looked like, could we?"

Munro said he guessed not and settle for, "Could I put him down as next of kin, in case something happens to me?"

The banker said that sounded reasonable until he heard the name. He stare morosely at Munro and asked, "Don't you know this Mister Culhane's real first name? Kiowa sounds sort of silly in a serious business transaction."

Munro nodded and said, "Let's just let it go for now. I may run into someone from the army who'd know his Christian name."

The banker looked relieved, handed Munro his passbook, and led him out front to pick up his cash. The younger teller who counted out the money seemed to know who he was, too. Munro was glad he didn't owe money or have some gal in trouble in such a nosy little town.

Munro put the money away and headed for the saloon as he considered how he was to get some of it out to the Lazy S. He knew that if he took it out personally Liz Stanhope was sure to argue with him about the price *he'd* settled on for the big blue and not-too-beat-up gear. He'd had the gelding long enough to know it was worth a lot more than ten dollars. The last time he'd seen a roping saddle at all like the one she'd thrown in, it had been in a pawnshop window, priced at twenty. He figured the very least he could owe her would be fifty. He knew she'd never take it if he tried to hand it to her. But he'd seen young Bob in town a couple of times since he'd been out to the Lazy S, and it was early yet. If he didn't run into the kid, he still might see Hank Mason or one of the other boys he'd gotten to know of late, and they could take it out to her. He didn't think she'd fuss at an innocent messenger.

He'd been drinking at the same saloon a good two weeks now, and old Trixie was looking better every time he saw her, albeit not *that* good yet. She didn't seem to be working when he entered the almost empty saloon. A cripple he knew vaguely as Lefty was spreading fresh sawdust on the still-damp floor. Munro nodded to the poor cuss but didn't address him by the only handle he knew him by. It was all too easy to see why some called him Lefty. His right arm was missing from the elbow down. He had to swamp and spread with just his left hand, whether he'd started out a southpaw or not.

Munro bellied up to the bar and ordered a beer. He got it. But when he asked the barkeep whether he'd seen any rider in town who might be passing the Lazy S on the way home, he was told, "Not hardly. Business is slow this far from payday, even when it ain't froze up outside."

Munro thought about it as he stood there nursing his beer. If worse came to worst, he could just ride out and let the fool woman cuss him. He wasn't about to take advantage of no widow woman who didn't know beans about horse trading.

The crippled swamper waited until the barkeep was serving a couple of railroad hands down at the far end before he came over to nudge Munro and mutter, "There's a gent looking for you, son. I said I didn't know where you was staying. I thought I ought to tell you first."

Munro raised an eyebrow and replied, "Do tell? Was he a dark-haired gent about my size, only older?"

Lefty shook his head and said, "Young and sort of runty, wearing white goatskin chaps and a black bearskin coat. He's packing an S&W .44 under said coat, double-action and cross-draw. He mentioned your name with a smile on his lips. But his eyes was not smiling worth mentioning."

"You think he means trouble, then?"

"I'm damn near certain of it. I've never seen him around here afore, but I've seen his kind afore. If he ain't a gun slick, I'll be switched if I can figure what *else* he could be. He's dressed expensive as well as cow. But he ain't no top hand. I had me a good look at his roping hand as he was pouring hisself a shotglass of expensive bourbon."

"Well, some top hands pride themselves in keeping their hands manicured and free of horn, lest someone take 'em for a common working stiff."

Lefty said, "I know. I used to *be* a top hand. There's still no way anyone but a tinhorn or a gun slick can keep his rope or gun hand so girlish, though."

Munro nodded and said, "I thank you for telling me, even if you're wrong. Can I buy you a drink, and what am I supposed to call you, pard?"

Lefty said, "I ain't allowed to drink on the job, and I'm used to being called Lefty, now. Lost my throwing arm nigh five years ago, and as a matter of fact, I can even write with my left hand now."

Munro nodded and said, "Seems to me a man who can read and write and stay sober on the job might be able to get a better-paying job, no offense."

Lefty said, "None taken. Working cows is the only serious trade I ever larnt. I never said I writ schoolbooks. I didn't make her past the third grade. I had little need for education, herding cows. By the time I saw what a limited future I had at that, it was a mite late."

Munro said, "I can see how that could limit your roping, old son. Do you mind my asking how it happened?"

Lefty said, "Dumb thing. It started as no more than a rope burn. I must have got cow shit rubbed in it. We was on a long drive, and by the time I could get to a town and a doc, my fool hand and arm was dead and all sorts of funny colors. So they had to take it off. The trail boss was nice about it. Gave me full wages, even though I was useless as hell for the last week or so of the drive. The outfit paid for the doc, too. So I had nothing to complain about."

Munro agreed, and Lefty went back to work before the barkeep could fuss at him. Munro finished his beer and had another. But nobody he knew came in. So he decided to go get some chili and come back later. He put down his empty schooner and stepped away from the bar, starting to button his sheepskin up again. He stopped and let it just hang loose when he saw what was coming through the front doorway, stomping snow off its boots.

Munro didn't know whether he'd have recognized Mister Death on second sight if Lefty hadn't tipped him off in advance. But the young gent in the white chaps and bearskin coat had the same expression on his lean and hungry face that Blacky Dawson had been wearing that night in this very saloon.

The stranger barely glanced his way as he called out to the swamper across the way, "Hey, cripple, has that Munro rascal been by yet?"

Munro thought it best to reach for his gun before he introduced himself and he was still cutting it too close. For the stranger reacted with astounding speed as he sensed movement out the corner of his eyes and went for his own gun with no more premeditation than a striking snake.

Munro was saved by the gun slick's bulky bearskin coat. The awkward sleeve threw its owner's aim off as he beat Munro to the draw easily but sent his first round through a part of the Munro's own sheepskin, where it didn't count. When Munro fired a split second later, his aim, or his luck, was better. He never would figure out where his second two rounds went, but the first hit dead center.

The heart-shot stranger fired once more, straight down into the floor between them, and wound up prone by the brass rail along the foot of the bar, with his hat resting on his rump and his face in an overturned cuspidor.

As the smoke began to clear, Munro realized he hadn't been breathing of late and inhaled a lungful of brimstone-scented air. As he began to reload, Lefty came over, stared down soberly, and asked, "Who was he, Mister Munro?"

Munro said, "Never laid eyes on him afore. I sure owe you, Lefty. Had not you given me an edge by warning me to look out for that shaggy coat, that would have likely been me on the floor at this very moment."

The same town lawman burst in, his own gun out. Lefty told him, "The one on the floor started it, Marshal." So the lawman put his gun away, saying, "I heard there was a growly bear in town. Why was he after you, Mingis?"

Munro said, "We was just trying to figure that out. I didn't know him."

The older man rolled the body onto its back with his boot, gasped when he saw the slime-covered face staring up at them slack-jawed, and said, "Suffering snakes, you're *good*, old son! You just gunned Sudden Sam Sawyer!"

Munro looked puzzled and replied, "If you say so. I still don't know who we're talking about."

The marshal said, "He must have knowed how famous

you was. He was a mighty mean bounty hunter and, some say, hired killer. Few lawmen thought it wise to try to prove that. He was so dangerous to mess with, they say John Wesley Hardin left Dodge the day Sudden Sam rode in, and it's a matter of record that James Butler Hickock in his prime refused to fight with Hardin!"

Munro put his reloaded gun away, saying, "I noticed he was sort of fast. But there ain't no bounty on *me*. He must have took me for somebody else."

Lefty said, "No, he never did. He was asking for you by name."

By this time other townsfolk had been drawn to the sound of gunplay. Their town marshal opined, "Whatever his reason, he surely chose the wrong victim this time. We knew you was good, Mingis. But you just proved you was better than the best in a fair face-to-face showdown!"

Another man chimed in, "He reads Indians better than a fortune-teller with a crystal ball, too! What we got here in a Medicine Wells is a boy nobody better mess with."

There was a chorus of agreement. Munro wondered if real gunfighters felt this dumb after a real showdown. It had begun and ended so fast, he was still confused as well as shaken. He knew he would probably get the shakes later, like the night after that sudden skirmish with some Arapaho, the first year of his hitch. The marshal's voice sounded sort of tinny and distant as Munro heard him saying, "It's starting to look like someone just don't *want* you here in Medicine Wells, son."

Munro said, "I noticed. I wasn't planning on staying. Now I got to study on that. I don't admire a crawfisher, and I'm sort of curious by nature. So I hereby proclaim, and you gents can spread it, that I ain't about to leave these parts until I am goddamn good and ready."

CHAPTER EIGHT

A February chinook Dull Knife should have waited for had burned off most of the snow by the afternoon Munro rode out to the Dorman spread again. June Dorman met him at the door to say, "My father had to ride over to the army post on business, and we don't expect him back this evening, Mingis."

Munro removed his Stetson and said, "That's all right, Miss June. It was you I come out to have a word with."

She looked flustered as she ushered him in, saying, "Heavens, the Grange dance isn't until next week, and to tell the truth, I didn't think you really wanted to take me. My father means well, but he can be sort of pushy."

"I wanted to take you," Munro lied, "but I ain't sure we ought to risk it."

She nodded soberly and said, "I heard you wound up with yet another unclaimed pony. My father and the hands were talking about it. Take off your coat and set a spell. I'll go put the coffee on."

He said, "I sure wish you wouldn't, ma'am. I come out here to talk, not to coffee up."

She said, "Come with me to the kitchen and we can both have our way."

He smiled, tossed his hat and coat aside, and followed her to her kitchen. It was big and well kept. Something baking in the oven of the big fresh-blackened range smelled grand.

She sat him at a table so lye-scrubbed the pine looked almost painted and said, "I can listen with my back to you," as she went over to the range and started poking up the fire.

He was glad he didn't have to meet her big old innocent eyes as he said, "The law in town has sent wires all over, trying to find out why Sudden Sam came after me like that. The marshal has come up with the odd notion that it might have been professional jealousy. He says some old boys just can't stand it when another gets a rep, and I'm sort of famous for shooting Blacky Dawson. Either way, anyone else out to gun me for whatever reason would be likely to consider that dance a fine place to meet up with me. So I hope you can see how it is. I'd be dumb to show up even alone, not knowing who else might want to ask me for a dance."

She put the coffee on and came back to join him at the table. As she sat down she said, "It was sweet of you to come all this way to tell me why you're not taking me. You were right about that black pony. He bucked me off the first time I tried to ride him. But I've got him broke to my side saddle, now."

He smiled and said, "I can see you're a woman of some determination. Would you be offended if I said I notice something else I like about you this afternoon?"

She looked puzzled. So he said, "You seem to act more, well, human, when your father ain't pulling your strings."

She sighed and said, "I fear my father is a mite strong-

81

willed as well. I'm not afraid of him, you must understand. He's never laid a hand to me, even when I was small and bratsome. But yes, I do have to watch my manners around him. He tends to lecture me afterward if he thinks I've said something silly. Sometimes I don't think he knows what I'm supposed to do or say, either. So it's best to just be his good little girl."

Munro nodded and said, "No offense, but a store-bought play-pretty fresh out of the box would be closer to the way you act when he's about."

She said, "I know. My mother died the first winter we were up here, and my poor father's been trying to figure out what I am ever since. Sometimes I think he'd like to keep me in a box, and other times I feel he's trying to marry me off and get rid of me. I cried in my room the first day you were out here and he talked that way to you. I knew you thought he was silly and I was just as bad."

He said, "I never took you for bad, Miss June. But seeing as we're talking more natural, I did feel sort of awkward."

"*You* felt awkward?" She sighed. "How do you think *I* felt, being invited to the Grange dance by my own father? I knew you thought I was just a silly little girl, and I thought you handled it awfully polite."

He said, "Well, I could see you was a mite young. But little girl would be putting it sort of strong, Miss June."

She said, "I'll be seventeen this summer. I don't think that's too young for a woman to be on her own, do you?"

He said, "I was on my own younger. But don't you want to stay here till you're ready to marry up, Miss June? Most gals do, you know."

She got up to see how the coffee was doing, or to turn her face from him, as she said, "I'm not sure I'm ready to marry up, before I've seen more of the world. I know my mother married at sixteen. She had me by the time she was seventeen. Then she got to live twelve more years, and then she was dead. I think she loved my father. I know he loved her and always treated her as well as he knew how. But surely she should have gotten more out her short life than she did. This world is so big. There's so much to see and do. There has to be more to life, even for a woman, than mama ever got to do or even see.

"I mind one time when I was little and she was reading to me in bed. It was a fairy-tale book, and I asked her what the seven seas might mean because I'd never heard of even one sea. She told me about the oceans far away. But when I asked her if she'd ever been there, she got sort of wistful and said she hadn't, but that she'd always wanted to go there and see what it was like. Do you think it's silly for me to want to see at least one of the seven seas before I marry up and settle down in some other sod house, Mingis?"

He said, "No. I'm sort of glad I got to see more than Texas before I was much older than you are now, Miss June. I've been up in the mountains, too. We got to chase Shoshone over near the South Pass, summer afore last. The South Pass country ain't all that different than around here. Just higher. But I've seen mountains with snow on top of 'em all summer, and ridden through miles of real forest. I know what you mean about old fairy-tale books. I mind one day on the trail, riding through aspen woods with the leaves all aflutter, and it come to me, then and there, that them green woods Robin Hood and his merry men holed up in between jobs must have been something like what I saw all around me."

She turned from the range, eyes older and wiser than he'd ever seen them before, and began to lay out cups and saucers as she said, "Oh, you do understand. There's this college back east that takes in women, and my grades were

83

always good when I was going to school in Medicine Wells. I've asked my father to let me go to that college. But he won't hear of it. He says my place is here, until the right man comes along, and that such notions just mess up a woman's head."

She went back for the pot as she continued. "Sometimes, when I'm alone out here with no company but the wolf wind, I get to wondering if marrying up wouldn't be the answer. At least I'd have *some* freedom, if I was careful about the gent I married up with. But then I get to thinking that he'd surely be a stockman. My father would never approve of any man who didn't have his own land and herd, and even if he was nice, I'd still be left alone with the wolf wind a lot while he was out on the range."

As she poured, he asked her, "Don't you reckon you have any choice at all in the matter? Seems to me a gal with such a restless heart would be better off with a railroader or even a gent with a job in town. They get home more regular, and I notice there's a library in Medicine Wells."

She sat down across from him. "The cake's not ready yet. I wasn't expecting company. I don't think my father would let a man from town spark me unless he was a banker or something."

Munro shook his head as she shoved the sugar bowl his way and said, "He has a point, you know. As a man of substance who no doubt worked for everything he has, he'd be worried about you getting stuck with a dapper Dan who expected to live off your father or, worse yet, let *you* live below your station."

She wrinkled her pert nose and said, "You men are all alike. I wouldn't mind, if the man was really nice, and we had to put off some of the luxuries until our fortunes improved."

He said, "Yes, you would. Women enjoy roughing it less

84

than men do. Any man with a lick of sense knows that. So any man who asks for a lady's hand before he's figured out how on earth he means to feed her and whatever kids may come along ain't no man in my book. So keep it in mind that Prince Charming is supposed to show up with more than one white horse to call his own. If he's a real man and not just a moonstruck boy, he'll have the mortgage on that castle all paid up. You sure make good coffee, Miss June."

She said, "Thank you. It's Arbuckle's, all the way from San Francisco. I know you own more than one horse. Do you have your castle paid for, Mingis?"

He laughed and said, "Matter of fact, I've been looking at some land now that the Pinkertons just sent me some more bounty money. But I hope you don't think I was proposing."

She said, "Neither was I. I'm not sure my father would want me to, since you've gained such a rep as a gun slick. He was saying just the other night that he may have misjudged you, even if you were from Texas. I don't think he'll be too upset when he hears I won't be going to that dance, after all."

Munro said, "No reason you can't go with someone else, is there?"

"There's nobody else to take me. I told you my father was sort of picky. A boy who used to work here isn't working here anymore because my father didn't like the way I smiled at him. He didn't do anything at all to get fired."

Munro grimaced and said, "I can see how you'd get to feeling lonesome out there. You say he's over to the army post tonight?"

She nodded and said, "It looks as if they really mean to close down that post this spring. Nobody else around here needs horses like they need breeding stock. My father says

85

he could make a fortune selling cows, if only he had cows to sell. But you can't even swap a pony for a good brood cow or he-brute now that the country's filling so with stock spreads. Where were you fixing to get your starting herd, Mingis?"

He said, "I hadn't studied on that. I thought it was more to the point to find a good site for a home spread afore I even thought about stocking it."

She shook her head and said, "You're going about it backwards. I was old enough to notice what my elders were up to when we first came up from Texas. I helped drive the ponies Father could buy cheaper down south. The first summer, this house was a tent. But we were already breeding, breaking, and selling horseflesh. The idea is to get money coming in, right off. You can always hire poor folks to drill wells, lay sod, and such. Father says that's why so many homesteaders go bust. They waste time building when they could be drilling in a cash crop. By the time they're ready to start earning money on a homestead, they've *spent* all their capital and one bad crop can wipe them out, see?"

He nodded thoughtfully and said, "The man that gets you will be getting more than a china-headed doll for sure. I confess I never learned much about business in the army, and even when I was working cows for other folk, I didn't study on the way they'd got started."

He finished his cup, shook his head when she offered more, and said, "Let's see, now. I ought to have the last of that bounty money come next month. March is warm enough to start driving down Texas way, and we'd be about two months on the trail, making it the beginning of green up when we finished the drive."

She gasped and asked, "Do you always think that big, that sudden, Mingis?"

He said, "I'm learning to. Thinking slow has almost got me killed, more than once. What's wrong with the notion? You just said there was a dearth of cows to fatten on the Goodnight grass, and down Texas way, cows are selling for two dollars a head and going hungry."

She said, "Oh, I think it's a grand notion. I sure wish I could go with you!"

He smiled wistfully at the pretty little thing, who had a brain after all, and said, "So do I. But we'd be coming back here. And your father would no doubt shoot me on sight, then, with good reason."

It wouldn't have been ladylike to track him into a saloon or call on a gent staying alone in a hotel room. So Liz Stanhope caught up with Munro as he was poking about the ruins of the Jennings spread a mile outside of town. As she dismounted to tether her buckskin in the dooryard with his big blue, she called out, "You don't want to buy *this* place, you idjet."

He said, "I know. But I promised the bank that owns the deed I'd look, at least."

She came through the waist-high doorway left in the half-tumbled-down sod wall of another man's dream and said, "They tried to sell this property to us when we first came north. A family called Jennings built this close to town because of the Cheyenne. They didn't build close enough."

He kicked at a lump of charcoal in the healing grass between the walls and said, "They told me how the bank was left holding the deed to this quarter section. Indians ain't the problem now. There ain't a full mile of open range to the south, and the town figures to grow into what land is unclaimed down there. I figured I'd start further out, with grass all around, not just three sides. The asking price for this place is cheap for a full quarter section. But I could do better with forty acres or less, given water and some shelter for my stock. Jennings must have planned on plowing the whole quarter section. It's flat and exposed to the wind from every quarter."

She said, "There's plenty of cottonwood draws further out, and you can drill for water anywhere in Wyoming and find it not too deep. That ain't what I wanted to talk to you about. Why did you send all that money out to the Lazy S with Bob Westwood? I thought we'd settled on a price, damn it."

He said, "You mean *you* did. I may not shave regular, but when I do I have to look at myself in the mirror, and I just hate a man who'd take an unfair advantage of a woman. Besides, I'm rich."

She laughed despite herself and said, "You can't hope to go on gunning outlaws as a regular career. What's this I hear about you planning to bring a herd of cows up from Texas, Mingis?"

He said, "Somebody has to. With the buffalo and Cheyenne gone, this grass figures to grow like Jack's beanstalk and choke us all to death. There ain't enough stock on this range to graze it right. I figure if I take half the money I've saved up down to west Texas, by train, of course, I can be back in no time with a starting herd. I'm looking to buy nothing but fertile heifers. A herd's easier to manage when it ain't mixed, in any case. I'll sell some of the stock to you-all and keep some as my own seed herd. I'll take your advice on letting 'em get into trouble ranging free until I've money to experiment with white-face bloodlines."

She said, "Makes sense. Then you do mean to stay up here, after all."

It had been more a statement than a question, but Munro nodded and said, "Now that I know as many folk up here as down home, I might as well. I may be slow, but I ain't stupid. If a man aims to make money, he has to go where it grows, and last I heard, cows was selling for two bucks or less down Texas way."

She nodded and said, "I said it makes sense. I admire your idea about leaving half your stake in the bank, too. It's a mighty long drive, and money on the hoof has a way of running off or dying on you."

He said, "The money I'm leaving ain't mine. I think I told you I had a pard named Culhane, didn't I?"

She said, "You did, but I'll be switched if I see how you could be pards with a man who ain't here. What's that ex-scout been doing to deserve so much consideration, Mingis?"

He said, "He's already done it. If I ever get really ahead, I figure to give Culhane all the bounty money on Blacky Dawson, if and when he ever shows up. I still don't know where he went right after the army fired the two of us."

She said, "Well, it's your money, and you've already proven to me that you don't know much about managing it. How soon are you leaving?"

He said, "This evening. There's a sundown train leaving, and I already bought my tickets."

She said, "Oh, I was fixing to invite you to supper. I reckon that would be shaving it too close, huh?"

He nodded and said, "I thank you for the invite. But I got a few chores to tend in town afore my train leaves. Mayhaps next green up, when I get back?"

She laughed and said, "I admire a man who plans ahead. I hear you didn't go to that Grange dance the other night, after all."

He said, "You heard right. I ain't much of a dancer in any case."

So she said, "Oh, I thought maybe that pretty June Dorman turned you down. I heard she wasn't there, either."

He didn't answer. She said, "Damn it, Mingis, did you or didn't you?"

"Do what?" he asked, even though he suspected he knew what she was getting at.

"I know it ain't my business. But if you didn't take her to that dance, did you take her somewhere else?" Liz asked.

He said, "You're right. It ain't none of your business. But since we're discussing a lady ahint her back, and she may worry about her rep, I hereby proclaim I never took June Dorman no place. You once said you didn't want to hear about it if I kissed her. But seeing you're such a suspicious-natured and spitesome she-male, I've never kissed her or been to bed with her. Satisfied?"

"Mingis Munro, is that any way to talk to a lady?"

"Not hardly. But you got to act like one if you want me to treat you like one. What's got into you, Liz? A man would think we was spoken for, the way you're carrying on about an innocent young gal whose only vice is hankering for higher education."

Liz blinked and asked, "A hankering for *what*?"

He said, "She'd rather go to college than marry up. I know, I thought she was dumber than that, too. But she ain't so stupid when her dad ain't watching, and you'd like her if you got to know her."

"Pooh, that stuck-up little girl and me got nothing in common unless you've been fibbing about your feelings for her."

He swore and said, "Damn it, Liz, when I want something, I come right out and say so. If I wanted to mess with either one of you, I'd just ask right out, so's you could say yes or no and that would be that."

She said, "Gee, thanks. It feels grand to be so wanted by a man."

He swore again and said, "Aw, hell, it ain't that cold in here, out of the wind, and the grass is dry. Would it make you feel better if I throwed you down right here and treated you indecent, Liz?"

She turned beet-red, ran outside, and forked onto her buckskin, riding off as if she thought the Cheyenne were about to strike the Jennings spread again.

He laughed and said aloud, "Lord knows what we'd have done if she'd taken us up on it. But she had a cussing coming."

He went out and mounted up to ride back into town at a more sedate pace. He said *adios* to the big blue at the livery, where they'd agreed to keep him at a fair boarding fee if they could hire him out now and again until Munro got back. Then he went to the saloon to kill some time before his train pulled out.

He was nursing a schooner of suds, alone, at the deep end of the bar, when old Lefty sidled up to him and said, "I hear you're leaving this evening for Texas. Something about a trail drive."

Munro nodded and said, "I studied on asking you, Lefty. But it would cost me another expensive train ticket. We'll talk about it when I get back."

Lefty looked confused and asked what he meant. So Munro told him, "I'm coming back with a herd and the least help I can hire, cheap. I figure any adventurous kid who can sit on a pony can drive cows in modest numbers. Once I have my outfit started up here, though, I'm going to need at least one experienced cowhand to help out around the place. I can't pay much, at first. But—"

Lefty cut in with a sigh, "Don't fun me, Mister Munro. It ain't right to hold straws out to a drowning man. We both know what I is today. There's no need to rawhide me about being useless."

Munro said, "Well, if you mean to blubber up on me, forget it. I don't kick a man when he's down for fun. If I can, I help him to his feet. I said I needed a segundo, not a roper. The kids you'd be ramrodding could have done the hard and dumb work. I was looking for a man who knew the cattle industry. If I've misjudged you, I'm just sorry as hell. Go on and bawl like a baby if you ain't up to working at something more serious."

Lefty's eyes were, in fact, filled with tears now. But he managed not to outright bawl as he said soberly, "I got enough for my own fare. I'm going with you, Mingis Munro. For if you think I mean to wait here with a mop in my one good hand until you get back from Texas, you are just crazy as hell!"

CHAPTER NINE

So Munro took Lefty to Texas with him, and it got more tedious than interesting for a spell. West Texas was enjoying a drought that winter, and scrub cows were dying on the hoof. But they'd heard about the rising beef market even in west Texas, so it tended to even out when he started bidding on anything that at all resembled breeding stock.

In the end they were able to scrape together only a little over four hundred heifers for close to nine hundred dollars. Lefty said the two of them could handle such a puny herd. But knowing how nice it felt to sleep once in a while, and seeing a twelve-year-old Mex and a fourteen-year-old Anglo who had their own ponies and were willing to work for their keep and a chance to see the world, Munro hired them on, trail-branded his modest herd the Rocking M outfit, and they were off for the Pecos.

They had no chuck wagon. Just the pack mules he'd picked up, along with a remuda Lefty was sure they'd meant to sell for glue until they'd seen Munro coming. He drove the cows hard the first two days, giving all four of them the chance to ride as hard and fast in every damned direction as their scrub ponies could manage. As Munro hoped, it settled the cows down so they stay bunched and docile once they were allowed to set their own more ladylike pace.

They followed the old Goodnight Trail up the Pecos, a lot slower than it takes to say something like that. They averaged fifteen miles a day in good weather and held the cows in draws when the Thunder Bird got to flapping. Lefty wanted to shoot a one-eyed cow he suspected of being a stampeder. Munro said everyone deserved a chance, and despite the way dry lighting spooked them one evening near the Conchas Divide, they managed to hold them together, even though the Mex kid's pony got hooked and limped some after that.

By the time they drove over the Arkansas Divide, it was only really bitterly cold at night and the two kids knew more about the life of a cowboy than they might have really wanted to at the beginning. They both wanted to quit more than once. But Munro shamed them, and Lefty cussed them enough to keep them and the herd going. North of the Arkansas it got easier for more than one reason. The warm spells between snow flurries were getting longer, and the Goodnight Trail was more clearly marked now. They could see others had been driving stock up to the new lush northern range. As they met a rider here and there or camped near nosy nesters, they began to hear about the others driving stock north. Some of the tales sounded a mite ominous.

So Munro and his crew weren't too surprised, or cheered, the afternoon they were fixing to ford a headwater creek of the South Platte to see a half dozen mounted strangers lined up along the far shore.

Munro rode on alone. Despite the early spring runoff, the creek was barely fetlock deep. He reined in within easy talking distance and said, "Howdy. If you gents is fixing to cross south, go ahead. Our cows can wait."

The burly, bearded rider who seemed to be the leader grinned wolfishly and said, "You got it wrong, pilgrim. It's going to cost you two bits a head to cross here."

Munro said, "That's sort of steep. Even if it wasn't, I fear you gents have made a mistake in setting up your toll crossing here. No offense, but this is federal open range. Nobody but Uncle Sam would have call to collect tolls on the Goodnight Trail, and your beard is just too black for you to be Uncle Sam."

The ruffian said, "As a matter of fact, they calls me Badlands Bill. No doubt you've heard of me, sonny?"

Lefty had ridden in close enough to take in the brag. Before Munro could answer, he said, "*I've* heard of you, son. Have you ever heard of Blacky Dawson or Sudden Sam Sawyer?"

Badlands Bill shrugged and said, "Sure. But ain't neither of you neither of them. We heard they both got kilt last winter, up Wyoming way."

Lefty said, "They did. And this here is Mingis Munro, the man who beat *both* of 'em to the draw."

They all looked sort of unhappy to hear that. But they held their ground until Munro said modestly, "Not both at once, of course. One at a time."

Badlands Bill looked uncertain but pointed out, "Anyone could *say* he was the famous Mingis Munro, and even so, it adds up to six growed men to one, a cripple, and two boys."

Munro nodded and replied, "I am glad you're good at figures, Badlands Bill. For here is how they add up. At two bits a head you are betting your life against a little more than a hundred dollars. I have no choice, because all the money I have is tied up in this beef. I may only get one or two of your afore you put me out of business, total, but you don't know which one or two it may be."

One of the others nudged Badlands Bill and said, "I think

95

he's bluffing." But the born bully had the instincts it took for his kind to get old enough to grow a beard. So he growled, "Shut up. I ain't so sure. A man willing to buck such odds for so little has to be either a lunatic or good. Maybe both."

Munro didn't say anything as the ruffian studied him for a long unwinking time. Then Badlands Bill smiled and said, "I'll tell you what I think, Munro. I think it's dumb for wolves to fight in a world of sheep. But I got my own rep to consider. If we let this drop, do I have your word as a man you'll not go about bragging that you crawfished the one and original Badlands Bill?"

Munro nodded soberly and said, "I don't see nobody crawfishing. Like you said, it just don't make sense for good old boys like us to fight. Would you mind taking your men out of rifle range while I get my cows across this creek, old pal?"

Badlands Bill laughed a lot louder than he must have felt like and yelled, "*Vamanos, muchachos*! It ain't polite to crowd an outfit fording snowmelt."

As they rode upstream Lefty heaved a vast sigh and said, "That was close."

Munro shrugged and answered, "Maybe. Somehow, after you've stared the real thing in the face, plain old thugs don't seem as scary."

Lefty said, "I hope we frightened them off for keeps. This new beef boom figures to be a pisser. It's already drawing buzzards in from all over. Come this time next year, the card sharks and fancy gals figure to outnumber cows all along this trail!"

But as they pushed on, Munro was more worried about weather along the Goodnight Trail than other dangers. The west Texas–born cows were still too nearly skin and bones to stand up to a late blue norther or even a blizzard. Munro could only hope he wasn't driving them north too hard or too early. He slowed the pace to an easy ten miles a day to graze them good on the ever lusher range, as the green up, or the peculiar substitute for spring the High Plain had to settle for, progressed.

Munro and Lefty were used to the green up, of course. The two kids from Texas found it as baffling as northeasterners more used to cold winters and warm summers might have.

For just when, or if, springtime came to the High Plains was a matter of some confusion. A warm chinook wind rolling over the mountains to the west could burn off a foot of snow, fill all the draws with muddy foam, and have everybody sweating on what had begun as a late winter day. On the other hand, a shift of the wind could result in a blizzard well into May, and, most dreaded of all, a wolf wind from the northeast could sweep in a cold dry arctic air mass, or blue norther, well into June.

As Mister Lo and his buffalo had known, and as many a nester was to learn, the grasslands east of the Rockies but west of, say, longitude 100° had been designed by Wakan Tonka for grazing, not easy farming. Few plants could survive the on-and-off spells of balmy bright sunlight alternating with sudden cold snaps and fresh snowfall. But the native shortgrasses and even a few introduced weed species could and did in fact commence to sprout new green growth, taking advantage of the rich moist prairie loam to get an early start and grow as much as possible before the soil turned back to brick-hard 'dobe no later than the Fourth of July.

Brush and even thrifty trees such as cottonwood and crack willow could survive the High Plains summers in the draws. So during cold snaps Munro sheltered his herd down out of the wolf wind where they could browse wild-cherry shoots and such. When it warmed up, he pushed them on across the open prairie, allowing them to gorge on richer grass than they'd ever tasted before as it turned emerald near the roots but was still cured enough from there on up to keep the fool cows from bloating themselves. They lost a day and almost lost some stock swinging wide around the beautiful sight of larkspur spreading a deadly floral carpet for miles across the rolling prairie. By the time they made the Wyoming line, the grass was Kentucky green and spangled with pale purple pasquel or prairie crocus as far as the eye could see, where the snow wasn't still sticking.

The weather held, and so, two weeks later, they made it back to Medicine Wells, where the Anglo boy sold his horse and saddle to leave for parts unknown. The Mex kid, Pete Robles, said he'd stay on at least until it got warm enough to ride on *sensible*.

So Munro recorded his Rocking M brand, cut a hundred head out for his own seed herd, and put the others up for sale. A beef steer worth not much more than two dollars in west Texas was worth ten in Wyoming. He asked fifteen a head for his fertile breeding stock and didn't let one go for less than twelve. So in the end he'd made a mighty handsome profit on his original investment and put most of that in the bank to draw interest as well.

Then he had to get down to serious work. The price of beef was not the only thing rising by this time. The old Jennings place had been listed at two dollars an acre a few short months before.

Now the bank was asking five. He'd thought it was too close to town in any case and settled on a full section farther out than either the Dorman or Stanhope spreads, for a flat thousand and no infernal bickering. The bank said they felt like they were giving the land away, despite the fact it was two miles off the wagon trace and all the cottonwood timber in the one draw running across the section catty-corner had been cut.

Munro had Lefty recruit some day labor at a scandalous

six bits a day, but found himself doing most of the work as they fought to put in the basic improvements before the ground got too summer-hard to work.

He drew his plans with pencil on foolscap and made Lefty in charge of putting up the housing while he and young Pete took care of the more important chores. The tramps Lefty had hired were willing to do some of the lifting and shoving as long as Munro or his hot-tempered young assistant stood right over them. The big blue didn't like it, either, but he was willing to pull as hard as any two regular ponies if you hit him enough. So they soon had a dam and water tank in the draw, and that meant the seed herd wouldn't wander more than a few miles out on the surrounding range for now. Munro knew he'd need a windmill to keep the tank wet later in the summer. But he figured it could wait until at least late June.

The tramps laughed, and even Pete asked questions when Munro had them run a ditch on the north side of the draw from one of his property lines to the other. Munro wasn't sure it would work, either. But he and Pete rode west a few miles to where the draw hadn't been cut for firewood. Then he chopped down young saplings and dragged them back to lie lengthwise in his ditch. While he was at it, they uprooted some chokecherry brush to toss in as well. Then he had his crew fill in the ditch, leaving branches of cottonwood and cherry sticking up to grow or wilt, depending on whether or not he was right. Munro explained to Pete that if it worked, they'd wind up with a shelter belt in a few years. The kid asked what happened if they got a real winter before the buried wood took root, and Munro told him not to be such a spoilsport. He said, "Only one winter in seven or so is a real killer up this way. On the other hand, sooner or later you got to get one. Once we do, it'll be too late to plant a shelter belt, see?"

Some of his stock had already discovered the delights of

the new swimming hole, while others were nibbling the exposed chokecherry shoots. Munro explained that was why he'd larded the more vital cottonwood with the tastier and faster-growing temptation. He said, "Down on the Brazos a lot of folk planted mulberry bush to keep the mockingbirds out of the fruit they really wanted to grow. Them choke shoots is almost impossible to kill off entire, and the stock will get tired of 'em soon enough."

The grass all around was in fact almost tempting enough for *people* to chaw. Lefty had fenced off a good-sized plot with wire to keep the cows out of it as he and his own crew cut sods.

There was some difference of opinion on the best time of the year to build sod walls. Some held it best to cut sods of summer-cured grass because grass tended to ferment when killed green. Munro decided to go along with Lefty's point that lifting sod when the roots were embedded in 'dobe hard as cement could not only get tedious as hell but tended to leave a lot of the roots in the ground. With the soil still green up soft, the sods came up thick and easy, with more wiry roots than grass stems. Lefty laid them roots up for the walls, and roots down for the roofing. You wanted the roof sods to keep growing and interlock tight. But grass growing out the sides of a wall not only looked silly but sucked the roots brittle before it all died and cured to a wall of hard mud and compressed straw. Munro warned Lefty to build it with ten-foot ceilings so they'd wind up with at least eight feet of headroom once the sod settled right. Lefty told him not to lecture an old hog on swill. Lefty was getting less and less humble as he felt his manhood coming back again.

Munro fenced in four acres of yarding around the main house and the outbuildings Lefty was building for him. he strung lath and bailing-wire snow fencing to the north and west to keep winter drifts at bay, and three-strand glidden wire to the east and south to keep cows from wandering in for supper uninvited. Cattle guards worked better in summer than under winter snow. So he built a regular gate. When young Pete found a buffalo skull and wanted to put it over the gate with the Rocking M brand painted on the white bone with black tar, Munro let him. It didn't look *too* silly above the gate, and the kid had been so proud of his artistic notion.

They had most of the work done, and Munro had let the hands from town go, with an extra bonus, the day Silas Dormer rode in alone on a handsome chestnut barb. Munro said he'd be proud to oat and coffee them but that he hadn't any cake to offer.

The older stockman dismounted but said he hadn't time to stay long. So as Pete watered his mount, Munro led Dorman afoot on a conducted tour of his new home spread. Dorman said, "I can see you put a lot of work in, and I'm impressed as hell. I always said I had you figured for a comer, Mingis. But that ain't why I rid over, either. You've heard about the trouble, of course?"

Munro looked blank and confessed, "To tell the truth, I've been too busy to get into town much. I hope you'll tell Miss June I ain't mad at her or nothing. I was hoping to have this place fixed up for a housewarming party by the Fourth of July, but every time I wake up, I remember something else I ain't done yet."

Dorman said, "The army's pulling out. I knew they would. So I've managed to adjust to that by selling off most of my ponies at some loss and starting my own beef herd. It figures to be a mite tight. It's sort of hard to build up a herd and sell beef at the same time. But that's what banks are for, and come fall roundup after next, the price should be even better."

Munro said, "That don't sound like trouble. Some say Little Wolf is up on the Tongue River now. But that's almost a hundred miles from here, and Little Wolf's fairly sensible, for a Cheyenne at least."

Dorman said, "We don't need the army to protect us from Mister Lo anymore. But with the outpost abandoned, we're sort of on our own, in unincorporated territory. There's talk of getting the federal government down in Cheyenne to issue us a permit to form us an incorporated county up this way. Meanwhile that's just talk, and meanwhile there ain't no formal law here outside the limits of the Medicine Wells township itself."

Munro nodded but said, "I don't see what the hurry is all about. We all know each other, and none of the outfits around here seem to be at feud."

Dorman said, "If we was only talking about neighbors we know, I wouldn't need to bank my money in town or worry about locking up at night. But the talk about a beef boom has strangers moving in. Some are just honest boomers, I'll allow. But both the Double Diamond and your friends at the Lazy S have reported missing stock, and I ain't seen hide nor hair of a couple of calves I was sure my own cows dropped just after that last snowfall."

Munro whistled softly and said, "My segundo, Lefty, said things tended to get that way every time the price of beef started to rise. But are we talking about trash whites helping themselves to temptation or serious cow thieves?"

Dorman said, "We don't know for sure. Like most folks, I was willing to write off a calf here and a mama cow there to natural wastage. But the widow Stanhope says her hired boy, Bob, spotted lobo tracks when he was out looking for her strayed or stolen critters. And the Double Diamond is missing a dozen head, and they can't see either a wolf or a trash white with a dozen kids to feed getting *that* greedy!"

Munro said, "Neither can I. But it's the wrong time of year to run beef into the railhead for sale. Do you reckon someone with a careless rope and a running iron could be out to start his own herd the easy way?"

Dorman nodded and said, "The notion come up at the

last Grange meeting. I may as well tell you that I have gone on record as a man who knows you personal and that you was kind enough to let me look your herd over, oh, let's say a few days ago. I know you ain't got any stock here but the stock you drove up from Texas."

Munro frowned and said, "That was mighty neighborly or you. But I reckon we'd both best take a little ride about my range, Mister Dorman."

The older man smiled, shook his head, and said, "Not hardly. I just said I knew you wasn't no cow thief. It ain't just because my daughter is sort of sweet on you, son. I know you wouldn't do a dumb thing like that because I know you're smart. Like me, you know how hard it would be to get away with such a thing while the country is still so open and the herds is all so small."

Munro insisted, "I still want you to tally my herd afore you leave. I don't know some of my other neighbors as well as I do you. They don't know me any better. It's only right that we set their minds at rest."

Munro called out for Pete, and when the boy appeared in the doorway of the sod stable, he yelled, "Saddle the big blue for me and get him out here pronto with Mister Dorman's mount. We're fixing to ride some."

Dorman kept protesting. But Munro insisted it was a fine sunny day, and Dorman had to agree, on condition Munro call him Silas, adding, "I ain't old enough to be your father, yet."

So a few minutes later they were on their way. Thanks to the way the sun had burned off all the puddles from the last snowfall, by now none of Munro's stock was all that far from the well-watered draw that afternoon. Dorman kept saying he could see a heifer was branded Rocking M even before Munro could cut and turn it for him. Munro had to insist before Dorman would ride further up the draw to tally the last few head, off Munro's actual holdings.

As they turned back, Dorman said, "Those are the ones you could lose first if you get hit. Thanks to your rep as the wrong man to mess with, they may pass you by entire. I know I'd go after Liz Stanhope's herd afore I'd mess with your'n, Mingis."

Munro said, "I'm sort of sore at her for not calling on us for help if she was missing stock. The Lazy S ain't more'n an hour's ride from here. But you say the Double Diamond is where they may have hit the hardest. That strikes me sort of odd, no offense. They got the biggest herd and the most riders."

Dorman said, "It struck me and some of the others the same way. On the other hand, the Double Diamond is further out of town, and it takes longer to miss cows from a big herd. Jim Harlow, of the Tumbling H, opined the rascals could have driven the Double Diamond beef due north, into still mighty unsettled country."

Munro thought and said, "That works, up to a point. Miles City would be the nearest market that way. Seems a long drive for a modest profit if we're only talking a dozen or so head."

Dorman asked, "Where would you run purloined beef if you was not so honest, Mingis?"

Munro said, "I'd hold 'em somewhere discreet until I had me enough to sell to balance the risk. Like you said, there ain't many spreads, official, once you get a day's ride out of Medicine Wells. But that ain't saying there ain't plenty of grass and water, along with lots of hidey-holes, in just about any direction you'd want to run a stolen cow. With the Indians moved out, the halfway-settled parts of the Goodnight grass are just spit in an ocean of open range."

"You mean an outlaw outfit could just up and run its own unrecorded spread, right out in the open under the Lord's blue sky?"

"Why not? It's a mighty big sky, and while it may *seem*

flat, this prairie rolls considerable. Up until last summer Mister Lo had whole villages down out of sight in many a Wyoming draw, and I know for a fact how hard it was to spot one from any distance at all. Poor old George Armstrong Custer met up with some say ten thousand Indians on a clear June day, in the middle of what he thought was empty country. Who's to say how many cows could hide out just as well betwixt here and just a day's ride or more?"

Dorman nodded soberly and said, "I said you was smart. You know this sea of grass good, too. Like I said, we're hoping to incorporate ourselves as a county, Mingis. You're a Democrat, of course?"

Munro shook his head and said, "Independent. I know I was brung up in Texas, but I've seen how rascals on both sides steal when folk vote 'em in without thinking. You take President Hayes, now. I know he rode for the north in the war and that there wasn't a Texas Democrat who voted for him. But fair's still fair. He put an end to the Reconstruction, busted up the Indian Ring that got so many whites as well as Indians killed, and so far he ain't raised taxes. So come next year I mean to vote for him, Republican or not."

Dorman shrugged and said, "I reckon most Texans would vote for a man they knew and respected as long as he wasn't an outright Black Republican, and, hell, half the townsfolk are damnyankees to begin with. The point is that if we're to become a county, we're going to need a county sheriff, Mingis."

Munro laughed incredulously and replied, "Suffering snakes, I just got old enough to vote myself. You can't be serious about running me for sheriff."

Dorman said, "We ain't. Caleb Norris has natural dibs on that position. But if he becomes the sheriff, someone will naturally have to fill his old job, see?"

Munro frowned and said, "Not hardly. I don't even know who Caleb Norris might be."

Dorman looked surprised, then nodded and said, "Oh, that's right. You was down Texas way when we lost our old town law and Caleb Norris was hired by the town council to replace the poor old cuss."

"I must have been. What happened to the old-timer? I got on pretty good with him as I recall."

Dorman sighed and said, "Everybody did. He got run over by a train one snowy night. As near as we could put her together, he was making his rounds late in the evening, blinded some by wind and snow, when he somehow wandered into the yards as the boys was shifting freight cars about. Nobody saw it happen. They just found him on the tracks in the morning, mangled considerable."

Munro frowned and said, "That don't sound right. I didn't know the man that personal. But he seemed sensible. I never saw him drinking on duty. And what would he be doing in the railroad yards late at night in the middle of a snowstorm to begin with?"

Dorman said, "You wasn't the first to say it sounded sort of strange. There was a considerable flap at the time. But it was a quiet time of the year, there hadn't been any trouble in town for weeks, and he had no known enemies. So it's just as likely it was one of them dumb things as happen around railroad yards, even to the boys who work there regular."

"Was this Caleb Norris gent in town at the time, mayhap looking for a steady employment?"

Dorman laughed and said, "You'll make a good lawman, Mingis. You're suspicious-natured as hell. But we had to send for old Caleb afterwards. He was working as a deputy clear down in Trinity, Colorado, the night the job up here suddenly became open. You'll find Caleb a good old boy once you get to know him. He's a pure professional, not just a natural bully who'd rather tote a badge than work. He'll make us a good sheriff when the time comes. But like I said, we'll still need a town marshal, and it's best to have a man who understands the way of a cowhand with a bottle, a six-gun, and a payday night."

By this time they'd ridden back to Munro's dooryard. As they reined in, Munro shook his head and said, "I don't want the chore, much obliged. A man raising stock this far out of town might be able to handle the lighter duties of a county sheriff as well, if the money was right. No way in hell I could run this spread and police the streets of Medicine Wells worth a fig."

Dorman said, "The job pays better than you figure to make out here with twice the herd, Mingis. Town marshal rates his own fine frame quarters, provided by the town, and, as Caleb Norris is about to learn, it's a position that can lead to greater things. Can as much be said for the considerable work you've put into this spread, with not a side of beef to sell, come roundup?"

Munro said, "There'll be other roundups, and I like being my own boss more than I thought I might. After an army hitch taking orders, it feels good to give 'em, even if only, mostly, to fool cows."

He started to dismount as he added, "I didn't just go to all this work to abandon it. Come on into the house and we'll see about that coffee I owe you."

But Dorman shook his head and said, "No thanks. Got to get it on home and see to my own chores. The Grange is meeting tomorrow night, Mingis. Do yourself a favor and be there."

"How come? I don't belong to the Grange, Silas."

"That's easy to fix. Come as my guest. With or without some regular law out here, we got to study on doing something about that missing beef, and it's best to be there when the boys get to choosing up sides."

CHAPTER TEN

The word "grange" entered Old English by way of Late Latin, and though it literally means "barn," it can mean "farm" as well. In the rural parts of these United States it had come to stand for an organization founded just after the war between the states as, more formally, the Patrons Of Husbandry, albeit seldom called anything but "the Grange" by friend and foe alike. Each semi-independent chapter met in its own lodge hall or barnlike grange. To do what was often a little fuzzy.

The basis of the Granger movement was a plan to better the lot of those who grew food and fiber for the rest of the nation and who often felt put upon by the city slickers who seemed to control the market for agricultural products, if not the weather and just about everything else that country folk felt vexed about. From its national headquarters in Washington, D.C., the organization issued suggestions, sensible or not, about agricultural co-ops, pending price changes, or hoof-and-mouth coming up from damn-it Mexico again. Each local lodge felt free to deal with its own local problems as its members saw fit. Hence the newspaper items exposing the Grange as anything from a radical Marxist movement to a snobbish country club devoted to fancy-dress balls and the discreet adultery of the horsey set. It all depended on who was talking about what Grange.

The one in Medicine Wells was too rustic to qualify as a club for country gentry, and like most stockmen, its member were far too individualistic to qualify as even Fabian socialists. Half the folk who showed up for meetings— some said the half that made most of the speeches—had never bothered to actually join the parent organization. Those who did pay dues often wondered why. But the barnlike Grange hall did serve as a grand place to hold fund-raising dances, cake sales, and such, and they could get more heads under one roof there than at the smaller town hall down the street when something of general interest to the whole community called for a get-together.

Mingis Munro found a seat against a back wall. Most of the more long-winded folk seemed to want their folding chairs farther out on the pine floor. He'd ridden into town with Lefty, but the older man had parted company with him outside. Lefty said he'd been to meetings of the Grange before.

As the meeting started awkwardly, Munro began to see what Lefty meant. There was a reading of the minutes of the last session followed by a full accounting of the proceeds of the last baking contest and cake sale. It was nice to know, but sort of tedious, that none of the proceeds had been stolen outright. An old gent in a rusty black suit reared up to raise a point and was told he'd have been out of order even had he been a paid-up member in good standing instead of a muley old windbag.

Then a muley old windbag who must have *been* a member in good standing got up to make a speech accusing the Jews, the Freemasons, or both of conspiring to keep Wyoming a territory just so that infernal damnyankee Rutherford B. Hayes could stay in office and oppress honest western folk with his infernal hard-money policy. Munro found it hard to follow as the First Lady, Lemonade Lucy Hayes, was further charged with refusing to serve hard liquor at the White House, and it was even harder to grasp what civil service reform might have to do with hard money. Munro was just old enough to remember all the trouble Confederate paper had caused his mother at the general store while he was waiting to grow up and fight for Texas. So he didn't see what was so bad about the government printing dollar bills backed by real gold and silver coinage.

He yawned and tried to pay more attention when another cuss got up to propose something called a beef cooperative for the local stockmen to join. Munro was a local stockman now, but he couldn't see how stock could be slaughtered and packed out here on the prairie so much better than it could in Omaha or even Chicago. He got the distinct impression the kind-hearted gent who meant to save them the trouble of dealing with all those useless middlemen figured to wind up as the only beef buyer they'd have to deal with. Munro was tempted to stand up and ask how they'd ever get one sole buyer to bid higher against himself. But he didn't. He decided he'd heard enough and that the boys over to the saloon would likely know as much about the future price of beef.

But he wasn't the only one there who was shifting about on a hardwood seat as if he was looking for the nearest graceful exit. The big shots seated up on the bandstand must have noticed this and decided it was time to get down to important matters before they wound up talking to themselves. The chairman cut the last speaker short and gave the podium to a tall, lean gent with a lantern jaw. He was introduced as Caleb Norris, the new town Marshal Munro had been told about. Norris was smiling down at the crowd like a school principal who wanted the kids to like him. Munro didn't think he liked the marshal much. Despite his smile, Norris had that look. The look of a man who suspects he's a wolf in a world that's mostly sheep.

The town's hired gun began by saying, "I'm not a member of your Grange, and, to tell the truth, I don't know all that much about raising beef or other crops. I'm a professional lawman, and as you all know, someone's been bending the law all out of shape in these parts of late."

He held up a sheet of paper but didn't read from it as he went on. "I won't take time to read off all the brands or tally all the heads. The point is that lots of you are missing stock, and we all know neither the wolves nor Indians are all that bad in these parts these days. As I was only hired to police inside the six- by six-mile limits of Medicine Wells Township, I may as well confess I've exceeded my jurisdiction a mite by poking my nose further out on the range and into the cattle industry than some of you may feel I should. So, right off, I want to know if anyone here thinks I ought to back off and stick to chasing the drunks off the streets and watching for chicken thieves inside the city limits."

Nobody said anything. Munro thought the cuss was acting a mite pushy, but it was a free country, and if he could ride into town, the town law had a right to ride out of it, as long as he wasn't bothering anyone decent.

Norris nodded and said, "All right. I'm sure you'll be glad to hear that as far as I can tell, none of your neighbors have been increasing their herds at your expense. I may not be a cowboy, but I know something about reading brands and how crooks run the same. I got the local brand book in my office. I've studied it some. None of you have brands close enough to each other's to change with a little hot-iron artistry, so—"

"That ain't so," Munro found himself calling out, even as he wondered why he had. It sure felt dumb to have a whole hall full of folk staring his way all at once.

Up on the bandstand, Caleb Norris was still smiling as he

called out, "Stand up and let's have a look at you whilst you tell a man he's full of it."

Munro got to his feet, calling back, "I didn't mean that impolitely, Marshal. I just meant it wasn't so that there'd be no way to run brands at all in these parts."

He saw Silas Dormer had moved over to say something in the lantern-jawed lawman's ear. He knew it was in his favor when the lawman nodded and called out, "All right, Mister Munro. They say you're smart about such matters, and I'm smart enough to listen when a man who may know more than me is talking. How come you seem to think someone could be doctoring brands too slick for us to notice?"

Munro moved closer as he replied, "I didn't say anyone here is doing it. I only meant it's wrong to say a thing is impossible unless you can show for sure it is. You take my own brand, the Rocking M. Who's to say I couldn't run the Rocking Eleven used by Mister Barlow, over yonder, easy by just burning his eleven into my M?"

An older stockman across the hall laughed like hell and called out, "I can. I ain't missing any stock, Munro. But I sure thank you for telling me where to look, if ever I do."

There was a chorus of laughter. Norris laughed, too, but as it died down, he said, "That's a mighty serious charge to make against yourself, Munro. Now that you've had your fun and shown me wrong on one set of brands, can we get on with the meeting?"

Munro said, "Sure. Go ahead. But by the way, it would be just as easy to run a Lazy S to a Lazy Eight, and that same brand book does have both a Double Diamond and a Slash X, you know."

This time nobody laughed. As the almost ugly murmur of confusion died down, Caleb Norris asked uncertainly, "Do you enjoy sowing suspicion among your neighbors, Munro?"

Munro shook his head and said, "Nope. I'd be mighty

112

surprised as well as vexed if anyone here has been stealing one another's stock. I only meant to point out it was possible. When you're out to cut a trail, you got to consider all the possible critters you could be trying to track. I once got in a whole lot of trouble looking for Cheyenne and finding Crow.''

Silas Dorman stepped to the edge of the bandstand to call down, "Who do you think we're all after, then, Mingis?"

Munro said, "I don't know. That was the only point I was trying to make.''

A stockman standing behind him opined that was the dumbest thing he'd ever heard in this hall, and he'd been coming here regular since it had been built. Dorman and Norris were talking more privately up on the podium. Norris raised a hand for silence and said, "All right, Mister Munro's point is well taken. We do not in fact know who's been picking off stock here and there, and I stand corrected. The question is what we're to *do* about it. I was about to suggest the formation of a vigilance committee to patrol the surrounding range and see if they can read any sign. Even if they can't, it seems to me a cow thief would think twice before he'd strike again with the range being heavily patrolled. If, say, each outfit was willing to send just one rider, taking turns, of course, we'd have us a permanent roving posse of forty to fifty armed and mounted riders guarding the range all the time. Any objections to that?''

Munro said, "Yeah. It would be unfair to the smaller outfits like mine, for one thing. The only rider I got to spare is me, and I'd miss out watching my own stock if I was way off somewhere else most of the time. It wouldn't work, even if we all had the riders to spare.''

"Why wouldn't it work?" asked Norris, not smiling at all now.

Munro said, "It never worked for us when I was chasing Mister Lo for Uncle Sam. Such mounted patrols are only

113

good for beans when they've cut a trail and have someplace sensible to ride. Just riding about in a circle, a mighty big circle, wouldn't do a lick of good and might well do harm. You're talking a diameter of sixty miles, since some spreads are out a good thirty and have cows ranging even wider. Leaving out all that schoolbook stuff about pies, you'd still be talking about a sweep at least a hundred and seventy-five or eighty around. Or almost a week of riding, just going around *once*, if they pay any attention to the range they're passing through."

There was an uneasy murmur from the crowd. Norris said, "I wasn't suggesting anything like that, damn it. I figured if they rode here and there, unexpected, they'd be likely to turn up most anywhere at any time, and that would discourage the cow thieves, see?"

Munro shook his head and said, "Not hardly. It seems sort of unlikely Mister Lo had spies in the army when I was riding with it. But they still managed to figure out where a large mounted force was, so they could strike somewhere else. We can't be talking about a very big gang of cow thieves. They ain't stole enough beef, yet. I make it no more than a handful of crooks, if that many, cutting out a head here and a head there. You go out after them, say, to the north, with all the gun hands they may be worried about, and they'll as likely laugh like hell and grab a calf well to the south."

Some others were starting to agree with Munro now. So Norris said coldly, "All right. We're all ears if you have some better way of dealing with the emergency, Munro."

The embarrassed younger man said, "I ain't sure if it's what I'd call an emergency yet. But if it was up to me, I'd worry more about where they're *unloading* the beef than the task of catching two or three riders out in the middle of so much nowhere. You're dead right about 'em not being able to sell a cow wearing its registered brand. Not to an honest buyer at any rate. So there has to be someplace, within walking distance for a cow, the rascals are *taking* the stock they've stolen."

Dorman called down, "I fancy your notion of a secret spread, further out, Mingis. There just ain't no beef being shipped, anywhere, this time of the year."

Norris nodded and said, "I didn't know that was *your* notion, Munro. That was one of the things I meant to have our vigilance posse look into. It might be a good idea to check with the brand inspectors further down the railroad spur, too. The rascals may figure to sell a mixed lot with made-up brands nobody has listed as stolen. In any event, like I said, we need some volunteers to do some serious riding. Can we count you in, Munro?"

Munro shook his head and replied, "Sorry. I'm short-handed as it is."

Caleb Norris stared down at him reproachfully and said, "We'll be in tough shape if everyone takes your independent attitude, Munro. Who do you expect to turn to if and when they hit your own herd?"

Munro shrugged and answered, "Nobody. I reckon if they mess with me, I'll just have to track 'em down and kill the sons of bitches personally."

That was about the way things stayed around Medicine Wells as summer came on more ferociously and water became more of a problem than the continuous but penny-ante stock thefts. Munro had his windmill up by mid-July, so his herd didn't suffer as much as some he heard of. He also sank a tube well, hand pumped, by his kitchen door. The more expensive and elaborate sunflower rig kept the pond in the draw filled to overflowing when the wind was steady. His stock enjoyed the green nettles that sprouted further down the draw, taking advantage of the once or twice a week overflow. As far as one could tell by looking, the shelter belt he'd planted had withered seriously by midsummer. But when you busted a twig with a thumb, the shoots still had a bit of life in them. It would take another green up to know for sure.

One day in August a young couple rode in aboard a buckboard, and as Munro made them welcome, they announced they meant to file a homestead claim a couple of miles away.

Munro said, "Well, you'll need water, and right now the topsoil is firmed up too hard for sinking a well without blasting powder. You're welcome to water your stock with mine, over in the draw to the north. Any time you need cooking water, feel free to use the pump out back."

The two nesters exchanged odd glances. The young gal still seemed uneasy. Her man, who'd introduced himself as Wes Garner looked more surprised than scared as he said, "That's mighty neighborly of you, Mister Munro. Can I take it you've no objections to us filing so near you?"

Munro said, "Come on into the house. I got coffee on the fire. Who on earth told you that you required my blessing if you aimed to file on federal land?"

As the young nester helped his wife down, he avoided Munro's eyes as he replied, "We know you graze your stock all about, and, well, we heard it said you was sort of, ah, testy."

"Is it true you killed two men in town?" his wife blurted before her man could shush her.

Munro grinned sheepishly and told her, "They was out to kill me, not to be my neighbors, ma'am. You'll find most of the folk hereabouts easy enough to get along with. I'll introduce you to some of 'em as you get settled. What are you figuring on trying to raise on your spread, Wes?"

The nester looked uncertain as he replied, "Thought I'd drill in forty acres of rye to start, if it's all the same to you and the other cowmen."

Munro sat them at his kitchen table and got out the plates as he said, "It's a mite late to drill in anything. But it's your back. If it was up to me, I'd put up a good fence first. At least three strands of glidden wire. Cows are sort of ignorant about propery lines, and so, do they see anything green sprouting this late in the year, they're sure to trouble it."

The girl, who said he could call her Betty, told him she'd heard fences got cut a lot out this way. Munro poured three tin cups of Arbuckle as he explained, "They might, if they're strung across a right-of-way someone's been using regular. I'd be a big fibber if I told you this was farming country or that all the stockmen around here admired fences. But, like I said, most of the neighbors is decent, and you two will have a lot more trouble with the weather, grasshoppers, and such than you will with any of us."

She demanded defensively, "Is that why you're so unworried about us claiming part of your range? Because you don't think we'll last long enough to prove our claim?"

He got out some raisin bread and said, "I'm sorry to say I ain't got nothing sweeter to go with that coffee, ma'am. Whether you make it or not is up to the Good Lord, not me. But since you're the one who keeps wondering what your new neighbors might think of you, I'd better tell you that you won't make many friends with that chip on your pretty shoulder. Sorry, Wes, but she did bring it up."

The young husband gulped, busied his hands with raisin bread, and said "We *want* to get along out here. Maybe we're a mite too anxious. We got dusted out in Kansas, heard there was more rain up this way, and, well, this is our last chance, and I reckon both of us are sort of worried past good manners."

Munro dunked his own bread as he nodded and said, "I noticed. That's why I mentioned it. Nieghbors get along, or don't, because they act like good neighbors or don't. Anyone who says he can tell decent folk from trash by the duds they wear or the cash crop they mean to harvest is suffering delusions of intelligence. If you find me no burden to settle a mile or more from, it won't be because I raise stock or string beans. It'll be because I don't bother you. That's all anyone sensible around here will expect from *you*. Don't sue nobody for grazing your unfenced crops, don't cut firewood off anyone else's land or help yourself to free veal chops that ain't been branded yet, and you'll get along all right.''

Wes said, "Good Gawd, we'd never do anything like *that*! Is that the reputation farm folk enjoy in these parts?''

Munro said, "There ain't enough nesters to enjoy any rep at all. But such things have happened in other parts. Folk used to the notion that anything fenced in is property, while anything that runs loose on public land is sort of wild game, free for the taking, can be a bother. Just as free-ranging stockmen who don't see no property line posted can be a bother to farm folk. So, like I said, fence afore you plow, and I'd try winter wheat instead of rye. You can drill that in as late as early October and reap her next June. Rye may be easier to grow, but there ain't much of a market for it. Are you figuring on a frame house or sod?''

Wes said, "Sod, of course. We haven't the money to even think about frame. Why?''

"Build small. Just enough to get you through the first winter. Late-cut sod will leak and dust you just awful, but it has to be warmer than nothing. Come next green up, we'll show you how to put up a bigger house that will last you better.''

Betty was starting to look less wary. It made her prettier. She said she was sorry she'd listened to the gossips in town and that she felt sure they'd all be friends. Munro said, "Aw, mush,'' and sent them home with a couple of buckets of water.

The next day Pete came in to say they seemed to be missing two head of breeding stock.

CHAPTER ELEVEN

The cow thieves didn't hit the Rocking M again that summer. Other outfits lost stock, however. So naturally the young nesters between the Rocking M and town came up as suspects, and Munro felt it just as natural to vouch for them. He had nothing but his instincts and the fact that they were new to go on. But when he pointed out that cows had turned up missing before Wes Garner even filed his claim, others were as fair-minded. It got back to the Garners that Munro had stood up for them. Betty embarrassed him by bringing over an apple pie big enough for an army. Worse yet, by this time she'd made friends with Liz Stanhope and asked Munro if he knew she was sweet on him.

He'd been too busy, or too smart, to call on either Liz or June Dorman, lest they bring up the fall dancing at the Grange.

He'd just got his spread in order, it seemed, when all of a sudden it was roundup time, and of course he had to pitch in, even though he had no beef to ship that fall.

It took the better part of a week, all hands working together, to round up one big consolidated herd, drive them to the cutting pens near the rail yards, and sort them out. Then Munro and young Pete Robles got to drive their own breeding stock all the way back and turn 'em loose again.

They'd lost another heifer. *Where* was a total mystery, since a considerable number of riders had worked together to sweep the whole range and tallied everything that looked at all like a cow. It seemed unlikely the brand inspectors working the cutting chutes in town could have sent a Rocking M heifer in with the big market herd my mistake. But sunset was coming on, and the buyers from the meat packers hadn't shown up yet, so there was no sense fussing about the matter just now.

Munro and his hands had just finished supper and were having coffee and a smoke for dessert when Liz Stanhope's young hand, Bob Westwood, tore in to tell Munro he was wanted, sudden, out at the Double Diamond. When Munro asked how come, the kid explained that everyone, including Miss Liz, was gathering out there to organize a posse. For just about every outfit in the area had tallied a head or so short by the end of the day's cutting, and a Double Diamond hand had found a small cold fire, likely a branding fire, in a draw just north of his boss's spread. Bod added, "Once we get everyone together out yonder, we mean to ride after the sons of bitches and larn 'em not to trifle with our beef."

"With the sun going down and no moon coming up tonight?" asked Munro with a frown even as he rose and reached for the gun rig hanging nearby. Pete Robles grinned like the mean little kid he was and commenced to do the same. But Munro said, "Not hardly, Pete. I want you and Lefty here to guard this place good while I ain't here. There's something mighty fishy going on in these parts."

As Bob Westwood followed Munro outside, he said, "Miss Liz says that if anyone can track on summer-cured grass, it has to be you."

But Munro growled, "Nobody tracks worth beans when it's the dark of the moon and the whole range has just been rid over in every fool direction. You go on out to the Double Diamond and tell 'em not to wait for me if they mean to ride in circles in the dark."

But Bob stayed with him as he went to saddle the big blue. So Munro had to explain, "I may be more useful where nobody else seems to be headed. There can't be more than one or two night watchmen guarding close to two thousand head, in one neat package, over to the railhead, with darkness coming down complete as well as soon."

The kid started to ask another dumb question. Then he proved Liz had taught him at least a mite about the beef industry that summer when he gasped, "Oh, sweet Jesus!" and added, "I'm riding into town with you. There's no way I could get all the way out to the Double Diamond and get back with help in time. The thieves would want to hit early and have the whole dark night to drive 'em hard and distant afore sunup, right?"

Munro tried to talk the fool kid out of it. But Bob wouldn't do as he was told and kept waving his old .36 conversion about until Munro muttered, "Put that fool gun away afore you blow a boot tip off, and listen sharp. If you have to come along, you got to promise to do just as I say, when I say it, hear?"

Bob agreed. So once Munro had his own mount saddled, with a Winchester as well as a double-rig roper, they were on their way.

They hadn't ridden far when they met the young nester, Wes Garner, along with a brother-in-law up from Kansas that Garner introduced as Don Forsythe. They were both mounted on scrubs but armed with decent repeating rifles. They said they'd heard about the big get-together out to the the Double Diamond and meant to ride out and join in.

Munro told them it was a grand notion. But when Bob Westwood told them they were on their way to save the big unguarded market herd, the fool farmers insisted on falling in with them. Munro had to keep going but said, "You got a wife, and you ain't lost stock, Wes. Nobody would expect you to ride after cow thieves, damn it."

Wes said, "You're wrong, neighbor." His brother-in-law chimed in, "I can see it's dumb. But I got to back Wes if he's backing you. We're kin."

Munro laughed and said he wasn't surprised to hear that from a man named Forsythe. It meant a man of peace in the Gaelic.

So they made it into town just at sundown, tethered their mounts in an alley within easy walking of the stockyards, and moved in the rest of the way on foot as darkness was falling.

It got dark fast when the prairie sky was so clear and cloudless. So they could hear and smell the pent-in herd before they could see all that much. A nervous voice called out to challenge them as they approached. The watchman on duty recognized Munro's voice and opened the shutter of his bull's-eye lantern. Munro told him, "Douse that light. Let 'em guess where we are. Who else do they have on duty here, Casey, ain't it?"

Casey nodded and replied, "Just myself it would be, until the kill-pecker watch comes on at midnight. What's up?"

Munro said, "I ain't sure. I hope I'm wrong. It's still one hell of a way to run a railroad. At, say, ten dollars a head, they have one gent, no offense, guarding more than twenty thousand on the hoof with a gawddamn lantern."

Casey patted his right hip and said, "Oh, I got my old '74 if I want to scare tramps. You surely don't expect anyone tougher to mess with that market herd, do you?"

Munro grimaced and said, "I can't think of a better time

and place to make that much money, honest or otherwise. Right now they have everyone in these parts willing to fight at all way the hell out on the prairie. They even have the town law out there instead of patrolling the town like he's paid to."

They were close enough to the pens to see the occasional glint of distant town lights on horn now. Munro turned to his tiny force and said, "All right. They ain't likely to want to ride in through town, of course. They won't want to ride over railroad switchings in the dark, either. I figure that leaves 'em an approach from the southwest, across open ground from, say, seven o'clock to, say, nine, if we was standing on a big old clock face. We'd best get over that way and take up our positions."

They did. Munro posted Don Forsythe behind a pile of railroad ties, put Wes Garner under even better cover by a toolshed, and sent young Bob up the ladder of a water tower so he could act as lookout or at least be out of the line of fire. He told Casey to stay with him and bring the shuttered lantern as he moved on to the cover of a loading chute running up to nowhere until someone had the kindness to provide a cattle car.

Nothing seemed to be happening. Casey said he sure hoped it would stay like that till he got off at midnight. Munro said, "Seeing we seem to have the time, hand me that lantern, will you?"

Casey did. Munro leaned his carbine against the loading chute and moved out across the dry grass beyond the ballast and weeds along the tracks. He put out the lamp, unscrewed the cap, and commenced to water the lawn far and wide with coal oil from the lamp's considerable reserve. He left just a little for the wick and moved back to rejoin the watchman before he struck a match and relit it. Farther out, someone must have seen the flare, for a distant voice called out, "Hey, Casey?"

123

Munro held the lamp low with its shutter closed as he told Casey, "Answer him, but keep your head down."

The older man called back, "Over here. Who's there, and what do you want?"

The reply came from closer. They had to be moving in fast. The one who'd tried to place the one watchman in the darkness warned him, "Just do yourself a favor and start running, old man. We don't want to hurt you. But we will if we have to."

Munro opened the lantern shutter and heaved it over the chute to crash and explode on the oil-soaked and dry-as-tinder grass.

Then he was shooting as fast as he could pump his Winchester into the milling gang of startled riders illuminated by the spreading flames out yonder. Casey, the two farmers down the way, and even the fool kid up on the tower platform opened fire as well. But in the tricky light they only managed to empty three saddles before the rest of the gang had crawfished back into the moonless night, no doubt chagrined considerable, judging by the awful things they were yelling about someone's mother.

It wasn't long—the grass was still burning—before the few men left in town with guns and hair on their chests came running to join the fun. But by then it was about over. Only one of the cow thieves on the ground was still breathing, and he refused to wake up no matter how hard they kicked him. Nobody there knew any of the owlhoots. But a merchant said one of 'em might have bought some canned goods in town, say a month ago.

By midnight all three of them were dead and propped up side by side on a slanting cellar door near the town hall to be admired if not identified by anyone who cared to be out that late.

By this time there were guns and lit torches set up around

the stockyards. So when Caleb Norris and all the others rode in around one in the morning, there was nothing left for Norris and his grand vigilance posse to do but agree Mingis Munro had been smart as hell. If Caleb's nose was out of joint, he was too good a sport, or too good a politician, to show it. He said he could see now what the plan had been. The penny-ante stock thefts had been designed to get everyone on the prod so they'd act as dumb as Caleb Norris allowed they'd just acted. He said, "They just drove that other stock further out to run wild on summer grass whilst we missed them some. Most of 'em ought to be drifting back to where they remember shelter, once the outlying range gets colder and drier. But where do you figure they meant to drive the main herd, Mingis?"

Munro said, "Like you said, to some other railroad stop. This time of the year, with consolidated herds crowding in all up and down every line, cows could be sold, cheap, and loaded in no time. The brand inspectors at each stop tend not to worry about strange brands when they're rushed and they don't have said brands listed as suspicious. The ringleader would have to know what he was doing, where he was going, and have a good story to tell, of course. But if he's known, local, somewhere else—"

"I follow your drift," Norris cut in, adding, "Come morning, I mean to send me some wires. We could be looking for a gent who contracted to ship considerable beef, somewhere, and all of a sudden didn't!"

CHAPTER TWELVE

It didn't work. On the other hand, Munro's slick move seemed to end all theft of stock around Medicine Wells for that year at least. With the surplus beef sold off, the remaining herds were easier to keep track of, and as the short Wyoming summer gave way to a long High Plains autumn as uncertain as its on-and-off green up, a man would have been a fool to try anything underhanded. It hadn't out and out snowed yet, but it could snow any time after, say, mid-September, and a thief caught out on the prairie by even a light snowfall would have no place to run to as his clear tracks betrayed him. So Munro was mighty popular around Medicine Wells.

As they worked to batten down the Rocking M for the coming winter, he found it hard to believe it had been only the better part of a year since he'd bought that arrow, it seemed so long ago and far away. So much had happened in so short a time. Hard work and healthy living had helped him get over the effects of his awesome wound by now. He'd always have the scar, and sometimes, after a long day in the saddle, he found himself a mite short of breath. Otherwise, he seemed strong as ever and mayhap older-looking, or at least more mature-looking than a gent his age was supposed to look. There was no other way to account for the fool notion some of his neighbors had about running him for their county sheriff in November, once all the papers came through from Cheyenne. He kept saying he was too busy. But nobody seemed to pay attention, even though Caleb Norris was campaigning for the same office, officially, with the blessings of the Grange.

Munro suspected his nearest neighbors, the Garners, and their kin, the Forsythes, were behind some of the talk about hanging a fool county badge on him. He'd helped both Wes and his brother-in-law switch to stock once they'd had time to grasp the harsh realities of the grass of Goodnight. Thanks to their now-famous standoff at the stockyards, they both enjoyed more standing in the community than one would expect newcomers from Kansas, and damnyankees to boot, to have. Worse yet, now both Betty Garner and Cindy Forsythe seemed to be conspiring to get Munro in trouble with women. Betty seemed to feel he was a fool to ignore the pretty widow Stanhope, while Cindy pointed out he'd do even better with the younger and prettier June Dorman, who was nice as well as rich.

He met both of them in town from time to time, of course, as the pleasant nights of autumn and the promise of snowbinding to come sparked the social season of Medicine Wells. He wanted to ride in and see what the Halloween ball at the Grange was like. But he didn't want to hurt anyone's feelings, and he knew folks were sure to talk if he tried to take both gals to the same fool dance. Later, he heard they'd both gone, alone, and sat as far apart along the wall as they could from one another.

He thought he was safe the weekday afternoon he had to go into town and draw some cash from the bank to pay Pete and Lefty. They'd both agreed to work for their keep until he had the spread on a paying basis. But you had to let a man or even a boy have *some* spend-or-jingle now and again. He put the money in his own jeans and drifted over to the saloon to get at least some enjoyment out of the trip for himself. It was a nippy afternoon, even wearing a sheepskin, with no longjohns under his jeans. As he bellied up, the barkeep said it looked like snow. Munro said he could taste it in the air and asked for some suds to get rid of it. It was too early for either the piano or Miss Trixie to offer distraction. But others were drifting in to warm up as the sky outside turned sort of ominous. Munro knew most of them, of course, and the few cowhands he didn't know looked friendly enough. It was getting harder to keep track of new faces as the surrounding spreads hired on more help and even newer outfits moved in as word of the grass of Goodnight got around. Munro spotted young Bob Westwood in the crowd. The kid was too young to be holding that big beer schooner, but since he'd taken part in a real shoot-out, he seemed to think he rated more manly privileges, and since he was packing an ivory-gripped conversion on one skinny hip, nobody seemed to care.

Munro drifted down to him, carrying his own drink, and said, "Howdy, Bob. Does Liz Stanhope know you're so far from home?"

The kid nodded and said, "I rid in with her. Miss Liz and the other ladies of the Grange ax-something-or-other are holding a powwow at the hall about she-male suffrage. I don't know why, but they seem to feel they ought to be able to vote in the coming county elections. You know how dumb she-males talk when they get together to plot against us."

Munro smiled thinly and said, "That's for sure. I got two otherwise pretty neighbor gals who seem to be plotting my ruination. You give my respects to Miss Liz, though, next time you see her, sober."

Then he moved on to see if there was someone more grown-up in the place to jaw with. A hand reached out to grab him by the arm as a familiar voice said, "Mingo, you old basser, are you still here in this bitty jerkwater town?"

Kiowa Culhane didn't look at all as Munro remembered him now. The erstwhile scout was dressed tinhorn expensive with a black fur collar to his fancy black greatcoat, and the pancaked black Stetson looked new and expensive, too. As his old army buddy hauled him over to a corner table, the two rougher-looking sorts who'd been sitting there got up to make room for them. Kiowa told one to fetch them a bottle and some glasses from the bar. As he and Munro sat down, he explained, "They work for me. I'm what you might call a field supervisor for a big private detective agency these days."

Munro nodded and said, "You told me you was looking for work as a hired gun. I wish I'd known you was in town earlier. The bank just closed a few minutes ago, and you got some money in it. Now we'll have to get it out for you in the morning."

Culhane shook his head and said, "I don't figure on being here that long, Mingo. We just blew in to do a little job this evening, and it's best to leave directly after such a job. But let's talk about you. I didn't know you was still in these parts. How did you handle that, ah, business we had with that other cuss in this very saloon that time?"

Munro said, "I stayed and faced the music, like you should have. He was a wanted killer. They wouldn't have arrested you for what happened. You'd have got the money posted on him. They gave it to me, instead. But I've been keeping it for you at the bank. It comes to close to fifteen hundred, Kiowa."

Culhane smiled wistfully and said, "You was right. It's too bad we met up after the bank closed. But let's not worry about it, Mingo. I'm making good money these days, and like I said, I don't plan to be in town that long."

The man Kiowa had sent to the bar came back with a

bottle and the shot glasses. He set them down politely enough but leaned down to ask Culhane quietly if he knew who he was drinking with.

Culhane said, "I do. This is my old pard, Mingo. We used to hunt redskins together." So the other man shrugged and moved off.

Culhane poured as he said, "I'm glad to see you looking so up-and-at-'em since last we met, Mingo. Does that wound ever bother you?"

Munro said, "No. Never mind about me. Who have you been hired to gun, Kiowa?"

Culhane looked injured and said, "I wish you wouldn't put it so brutal, Mingo. Like I told you, I ain't a hired killer. I'm just a sort of troubleshooter. I got a gun permit, and I'm licensed by my agency, just like a regular lawman, see?"

"I know how it works. It must be just awful to have suspects resisting arrest on trumped-up warrants. Of course, if they didn't, they'd get off in any court of law, right?"

Culhane chuckled and said, "Brutal or not, you do know how the law can be sort of bent to fit, albeit, like I said, I usually find it best to just leave town afterwards."

"I said I knew why you come to Medicine Wells, Kiowa. I still want to know *who*. Most of the boys around here are friends of mine."

Culhane raised an eyebrow, raised his glass as well, and said, "To your continued good health, and I mean that, Mingo. I don't know who it is, yet. I got to meet someone here who sent for our help. It won't matter to you who it is, if you have any sense at all. You know how fond I am of you, old son. But business is business, and you know better than to try to stop me."

Munro left the drink in front of him untouched as he said soberly, "I may not have any choice. I suspicion I know who they sent you to gun."

"Do tell, Mingo? Who might that be, and is he any good?"

Munro said, "Not as good as you. We both know that. But just the same, it figures to be me."

"You?" Culhane frowned, adding, "Now why in thunder would anyone want to treat *you* so mean, Mingo?"

Munro said, "I make crooks nervous. I've been nominated for county sheriff, and that would likely make them even more so. I know better than to ask who you're working for. But could I ask one favor for old time's sake?"

Culhane nodded but said, "Let's not get our bowels in an uproar just yet. I don't know who I'm gunning for, yet."

Munro said, "That's all right. I do. It's crowded in town right now. There's no way we can shoot it out without risking all sorts of grim accidents. What if I was to wait for you in some more secluded place? That way I wouldn't have to worry about my friends and you wouldn't have to worry about witnesses, see?"

Culhane nodded soberly and said, "That sounds fairer to me than you, Mingo. Let's hope it ain't you they want me to take care of. But in case it is, just when and where did you have in mind?"

Munro said, "There's a burnt-out soddy, the old Jennings place, just a mile outside of town to the north. The walls might keep the wind off me enough to stop me from freezing stiff if I was to wait for you out there, say about sundown? You'll know for sure by then, right?"

Culhane nodded but said, "I dunno, Mingo. Seems to me that even you might have a chance against me if I let you fort up in advance in a ruin and then rode at you like a big-ass bird."

Munro said, "You have my word I'll step out in the open the moment I see you coming. I'll know who you're after, of course, if and when you do. So we won't have to shilly-shally. It'll be just you and me, out there alone, even money."

Culhane sighed and said, "Not hardly. I've seen you in

131

action, and you've seen me. You wouldn't have a chance against me in such a fair fight, old son. So I got a better idea. What say you just start running afore I get word about you one way or the other?"

Munro said, "I don't run as good as you, no offense. Try her another way. I told you I have some money in the bank. What if I was to offer all I had to you? You can't get that much for just one killing, damn it."

Culhane said, "Not hardly, and I have to split the fee with my backup, whether they take part in the shoot-out or not. But that ain't the point, Mingo. Once I've been sent out on a job, my outfit expects me to do it. How would it look, professionally, if word got about that Kiowa Culhane could be bought off at the last minute?"

"I can see you value your professional standing," said Munro dryly. Then he shrugged and said, "You just intimated you wasn't afraid of me in a stand-up fight. So do we have us a deal?"

Culhane said, "I hope not. I like you too much. But if it is you, and I do come after you alone, on your own terms, do I have your word as a man you won't be forted up in them ruins with a full platoon of friends?"

Munro nodded soberly and said, "I told you I didn't want none of my friends hurt, and I've seen how good you are at hurting folk."

"How come you ain't afraid, then, Mingo?"

"I am afraid. I never was as dumb as you. But it's like when you're stuck with a toothache. You can piss and moan and try all sorts of things that don't really help, or you can make yourself an appointment with the dentist and get it over with."

Culhane laughed almost boyishly and said, "You've grown up some since last we met. I sure hope you get to wait out there for me in vain, Mingo. For do you see me coming, you'll know I ain't coming to pull your fool teeth!"

CHAPTER THIRTEEN

It was too late to change the way it had to be by the time it started snowing hard that afternoon. Munro had left the saloon directly after promising to wait at the Jennings place, of course, since he knew he didn't have much of a chance against Culhane cold sober. He was at the smithy, seeing to the big blue's shoes, when the first flakes started to drift down from the slate-gray sky and the blacksmith opined they were in for it, sure as hell. By the time Munro got back to the saloon, it was even more crowded, but Culhane was not to be seen.

On his way back to his horse he ran into June Dorman and another young gal on the sidewalk. She laughed and asked if he didn't find the early snowfall delightful. He said he didn't see what was so laughable about it, and she confided she was fixing to stay in town with the other gal, Shirly, because her father had told her not to risk riding home in a blizzard if his nose was right about snow in the air. Shirly added that they meant to make some taffy at her house and that he was welcome to come along and pull it with 'em if he had nothing better to do.

He ticked the brim of his hat at them both and said they had no idea how much he felt like pulling taffy right now but that he had less delightsome business to attend to before he could have fun. He asked how the suffrage meeting at the Grange had gone, and they both made faces and June said nothing had been settled, save that some of the old biddies there sure liked to talk and seemed to hate men more than she and Shirly did. He laughed and sent them on their way to pull taffy and likely gossip about him. He wondered how long either would remember him if he was right about the reason his old army buddy was in town.

He forced himself to kill more time in town, knowing how cold it would be out on the prairie right now and wondering as he did so why on earth a man would feel so anxious to ride out and get it over with. He knew his only hope was the outside chance that Kiowa could be after someone else. He went over the deal they'd made, over and over again, looking for some possible edge he could manage. Nothing had been said about a quick-draw contest. Kiowa couldn't say it was dirty if he just stepped out with his Winchester, as long as he did so at honest range. Kiowa would know better than to come out with just his side arms. So they'd both be set to fire at, say, a hundred yards. Maybe closer if this snow kept up. Whether at close range or far, Kiowa was a better shot with anything that fired. But a deal was a deal, and what the hell, one round in a hundred misfired or jammed, right?

The next time Munro saw a clock in a shop window, he was surprised to see how time could fly when a man wasn't sure how much he might have left. He sighed, went back to the smithy, and got the big blue.

As they rode out of town, he knew the sun had to be still up somewhere, but it was hard to prove. There wasn't much wind. But the snow was coming down seriously, and the wagon trace was already covered with almost an inch of it.

He could see the faint tracks of someone else who'd ridden out after the snowfall started. The hoof marks were already filled in with fresh snow and starting to smooth over. That was something to study on. Culhane had been the one to point out the advantage of laying for someone, well forted up, ahead. But as he reached the old Jennings spread, he saw the earlier rider, whoever it was, had passed on up the trace without even reining in for a look-see at the old ruins. As he turned off the trace, he looked back to see what clear prints his own mount was leaving in the fresh fall. He hoped nobody else would come by, ahead of the real thing. He wasn't up to explaining what on earth he was doing in a house with no roof at a time like this.

He dismounted inside the sod walls. He started to look for something to tether his pony to. He decided not to. The big blue might wander home without him later, and if Pete or Lefty backtracked, they might find him before he was too stinky.

He got out his saddle gun and checked his pocket watch. It was already later than he'd wanted it to be. He was cold and scared, and if he didn't watch out, he was fixing to start crying.

He swore, called himself a big baby, and tried to get his mind off dying by considering who might want him dead. That did kill some more time but didn't get him anywhere. He could see now that the cow thieves they'd driven off had to be in with someone local. That accounted for where they'd holed up when they hadn't been skimming the surrounding herds to put everyone on the prod. After that it got more mysterious. He didn't think Caleb Norris liked him. He knew he didn't like Norris. But to be fair, old Caleb had shown up after the trouble had started. He'd been sent for, by whom? To fill in for the old lawman, who'd died sort of odd as well as sudden, come to study on it.

Munro blew into his cupped hands to warm them and

muttered aloud, "Yeah, we'd best have a serious talk with old Caleb, if we live that long." Then he grimaced, laughed a graveyard laugh, and asked himself how he expected to manage that.

He had no answer when he heard a distant voice call out his name. He gulped, checked the chamber of his Winchester, and stepped out into the open, peering into the fuzzy gray haze to his south as he called back, "Over this way, Kiowa. Was I right?"

He could see a distant indistinct blur now as Culhane called back, "Would I be out in this weather if I didn't have to be, old son? I'm sorry, Mingo. But you just ain't as popular in these parts as you might have thought you was. Are you all set, old pard?"

Munro announced he was set as he'd ever be and waited on the wagon trace, his own gun at port, as the blur out to kill him commenced to get bigger. When he judged the range at about fifty yards and still hard to make out, Munro raised the stock of his Winchester to his shoulder and tried, in vain, to center his sights on the oncoming outline. But it was no go in this tricky light. He could see his sights, or he could see Culhane's ghostly form out there. He couldn't get them both in focus at the same time. He started to squeeze the trigger. His finger refused to move. He didn't know whether it was the cold or buck fever. He only knew he was holding his fire too damned long and that any moment . . . Then the snow-filled air was rent by the sound of a single rifle shot, and then Munro was able to fire, lever his Winchester, and fire again, even as he wondered dully why he was still on his feet.

He'd lost track of Culhane now. The gun slick was down, hit or not. Munro crabbed sideways to flop belly-down in the snow-filled ditch by the side of the wagon trace, his heart pounding and his ears straining. It snowed on quietly for a million years. Then he heard Culhane call conversationally, "Hey, Mingo?"

"Yeah?" Munro replied cautiously.

"You got me. Good. How the hell did you *do* that, old son?"

"Just lucky, I reckon. If it's over, I could get a doc for you, Kiowa."

Culhane called back, "It's over. I don't need a doc. But I sure would like to die more comfortable, out of this damned old snow. You say there's a house around here, Mingo?"

Munro got cautiously to his feet as he replied, "Part of one, leastways. How do I know I'll live through it if I try to help you over to the walls, Kiowa?"

"Oh, hell, have I ever done you dirty, Mingo? I said it was over. What sense would there be in trying to take you with me now that you've won? In a way I'm sort of proud of you, kid. But no shit, I'm getting drifted over entire by this infernal snow."

Munro started forward, saying, "Keep talking so I can find you, then."

Then he froze as yet another familiar voice called out, "Don't do it, Mingis! It could be a trick!"

"Who the hell is that?" Culhane called out.

Munro was almost as confused as he yelled, "Where are you and what are you doing out here, Miss Liz?"

So Liz Stanhope replied, demurely as well as unseen, "Trying to keep you from committing suicide, you damned fool. Bob Westwood told me about this stupid deal you two made. Little pitchers have big ears. What on earth got into you tonight, Mingis Munro?"

Culhane answered for both of them, saying, "So that was *you* I heard firing off to the side? You missed me, ma'am. But I reckon you threw me off enough for Mingo to get off a better shot. Is she pretty, Mingo?"

Munro said, "As a matter of fact, she is. I know you'll find this hard to buy, Kiowa, but the lady wasn't invited to this party."

Culhane replied, "I never said you played me false, and we can't expect women to abide by any code. Do you love this boy, pretty lady?"

There was a long moment of silence. Then Liz moved in close enough that Munro could barely make her out as she replied soberly, "I reckon I must. I damn near froze my tail off laying for you off the trace in the snow."

Culhane laughed weakly and said, "It's all right, then. All's fair in love and war. Are you going to get me out of this damn ditch or not, Mingo?"

Munro told Liz, "Cover me. He's never lied to me in the past."

She told him he was a damned fool again. But a few minutes later the three of them were huddled inside the sod walls of the old Jennings place, and when Munro struck a light to see how badly Culhane was hit, the wounded man smiled gallantly up at Liz to say, "By Jimmies, ma'am, you *are* pretty as a picture, and that helps some. I'd sure hate to think I'd been kilt by *ugly* folk. You'd best marry up with her quick, Mingo. Good-looking gals willing to back a man in a gunfight are scarce as hell."

Munro said, "Never mind about my infernal love life. I got to tell you true that you're bleeding bad, internal. So you'd best get straight with your maker whilst there's still time."

Culhane laughed weakly and replied, "No Lord *I'd* want to talk to would have let Mister Lo treat my mother and baby sister the way they was found, and I've never done anything I was ashamed of since. I didn't figure on living forever, and this is a sort of romantical ending when you study on it. I do have one last favor to ask of you, though, Mingo."

Munro told him to name it. So he said, "If you was serious about that money you was holding for me, I'd surely admire having the fine funeral I figured I might. Promise me

138

a decent send-off, with flowers, music, and all, and I'll forgive you this pretty wild card in the deck."

Liz said, "He never knew I was sitting in, Mister Culhane. I rode on by and then circled back, lest either of you spot my pony tracks, see?"

Kiowa nodded and said, "I ain't talking to you, pretty lady. Do we have us a deal, Mingo?"

Munro nodded and said, "Store-bought box and a grand granite headstone, do I live long enough to manage that, Kiowa. The odds on my doing so might go up if you'd see fit to tell us who you was working for."

But Culhane said, "That wouldn't be professional. They may send away for outside help again. But you don't have to worry about my own personal backup, Mingo. I told the boys I was after you fair and square and that they was to stay out of it no matter which way it went."

He added modestly, "They'd be dumb as hell going after any man who could take me, and they know it. Is the snow letting up, or am I just feeling less with my fool face?"

Munro said, "Both, I reckon. The sky does look a mite clearer, but let's talk about others who might be coming for me, Kiowa. Can't you even give us a hint?"

"Not hardly. You know I've always been a man of my word. Your best bet would be to take this pretty lady by the hand and move clean out of the territory. I *can* tell you they're after you because you've been getting in their way. It ain't personal. I know this because I asked, once they told me who they wanted me to gun for 'em."

Munro grimaced and replied, "I couldn't help taking it sort of personal when they kept sending hired killers after me. I mean ahead of *you*, no offense."

Culhane shook his head and insisted, "I was the first gun they hired direct. You was there when that Blacky Dawson just started up with the both of us to prove he was loco. They told me they was surprised as you was by the surly manners of that second one, Sawyer. He'd been turned down as a loose cannon by the wiser heads who hired me. He proved how wise they was by going after you on his own. He must have wanted to add to his rep by taking out the only gent in these parts with a rep of his own. My point is that the gents who hired me and my boys ain't out to avenge a thing but your rude habit of getting in the way every time they aim to purloin some local beef. So it's safe to assume that once you leave, they ain't likely to come after you."

Munro didn't answer. Liz said, "I ain't running, neither."

Munro shushed her and murmured, "Keep your voice down. I think I just heard something."

He had. A few moments later all three of them heard a rough voice call out, "Hey, Culhane? Your horse is here. So where in hell might you be?"

Culhane struggled to sit up straighter as he called back, "Go on back to town, Windy. I told you not to mix in this, damn it!"

He added in a softer growl, "Good help is sure getting hard to find these days. Somebody get me on my damn feet. I can't seem to feel 'em so good right now."

Munro told Liz, "Keep him still," as he moved to the nearest gap in the sod walls.

It was hardly snowing now, but it was still too dark to see anyone out there as the same voice called back, "Client's orders, Culhane. He didn't like it much when he heard about the deal you made. He says he paid to have Munro done in, not to add to his rep. Are you all right? Your voice sounds funny, like you was down in a hole."

Culhane called back, "I'm shacked up with a prairie dog, and I still want you to back off, Windy!" Then he told Liz, "Help me up, damn it! Windy's smart as well as mean. There's two of 'em, and Spud may already be working around to hit you from the side as Windy moves in more noisy, see?"

She started to haul him up the inside of the wall but asked him, "How do I know we can trust you? Why would you want to change sides, anyway?"

He grinned boyishly at her and said, "I've had a .44 Lighting under this coat all this time, pretty lady. I ain't never been on any side but my own, and I'm holding you both to that proper funeral, hear?"

Then he wrenched free of her and staggered outside, yelling, "Here I am, and what in thunder's got into you boys tonight? I thought it was understood *I* was in command of this operation, and if *you* mean to be boss, you'd better just fill your fist, Windy!"

Then all hell broke loose. Neither Munro nor the girl crouched beside him with her carbine cocked could make out anything but dull orange flashes of muzzle blast against the blackness for a short but noisy spell. Then it got very quiet. Liz whispered, "Don't call out to him. If they don't know where we are, they may not rush us."

He said, "Cover the back." She moved away to do so, and it got even quieter. It felt like they'd waited hours before the eastern horizon began to lighten. It took even longer for a big fat harvest moon to come up for a surprised look at its autumn prairie white with snow. As the light got better, Munro told Liz softly, "I can see three man-sized dark spots out my way. What about you?"

She answered, "Nothing but snow, as far as a mile or more. Didn't he say there was two of 'em?"

Munro said, "Two backups as came here with him. That ain't saying they come looking for him alone. The one called Windy mentioned surly suspicions from the local rascal they was hired by. I don't see no riding stock out there. Where did you leave your own mount, Liz?"

She said, "Tied to a willow in a draw, to the west."

"Do tell? I don't recall anything that deep near this old soddy, Liz."

"There ain't. It's about half a mile out. I said I like to have froze my tail off, crawling through the snow like a durned old Cheyenne. But someone has to look after a muley man without a lick of sense."

He nodded soberly and said, "I reckon I owe you. There ain't no stock out there now. Their mounts must have all been spooked by the gunplay and run off. Unless one of the gents out there is acting mighty sneaky, I reckon we're in the clear."

She said, "I'm cold. Put a round in each one to make sure and let's get out of here, damn it."

He started to object. But there was nothing wrong with her logic. So he took aim in the improved light, and nobody out there moved when they got shot again. Munro stood up and joined Liz near the rump of the big blue to say, "I'll ride you double to your own critter. Then I want you to go on home."

"I will if you'll come with me. We've both heard enough noise for one evening, Mingis, and I just baked a cherry pie."

He didn't answer. She waited until they were riding the big blue double across the moonlit snow before she asked, "If you don't like my baking, what else might you have in mind?"

He said, "Tracking. If you was a horse without a rider, on a night like this, would you just wander about cold and hungry or head for your home stable?"

She said, "That might work if those gun slicks didn't hire livery nags in town when they got off the train."

He said, "They didn't. I asked. I was looking for Kiowa in town to postpone our showdown when it started snowing. So it seems more likely they borrowed all three ponies off the rascal who sent for 'em. Nobody could have planned on even one of those horses heading home by moonlight across virgin snow. But that's what happened, and the trail ought to be clear enough for a schoolgal to follow."

She said, "I ain't a schoolgal, but I'm packing a carbine, and I'll be surprised as hell if them pony tracks lead to any schoolhouse, anyways. You can't go after them alone, Mingis."

He said, "Sure I can. I have to. By the time I could gather enough help to matter, assuming I knew who to trust right now, other stock could mess up them pony tracks on me. There's no wind. It ain't cold enough to keep range stock sheltering in the draws forever. So I got to trail whilst the trailing is good."

She called him a mule-headed fool again but didn't press it until they'd made it to the willow-choked draw she'd left her own mount sheltered in, and he got to notice how he felt down the front now, with her warm body aboard another saddle.

He thanked her again for saving his life, told her to get on home now, and thought that was the end of it until he noticed she was riding with him as he headed back to the wagon trace. He asked where she thought she was going, and she said, "With you, of course. I know the two of us won't be enough. They'll surely fort up and lay for us the minute they see that riding stock come in with empty saddles. But two is twice as much as one, and if you say I'm just a fool girl again, I'll spit."

He laughed and said, "All right, on one condition. When and if we track them ponies to the den of the skunk ahint all this, I'll expect you to ride for help while I keep 'em pinned down. I'd best not send you into town for help, even though it's closer. If you ride toward my spread, you can trust Wes Garner and Don Forsythe, as well as Lefty and young Robles. Four men, a boy, and one mighty tough she-male ought to be able to handle any outfit who sends away for its own fighting. They may not have the grit to fight at all, knowing we was good enough to lick their mail-order guns."

She agreed that sounded sensible. They got back to the scene of the carnage, and he dismounted to circle for sign. None of the bodies had much to tell him. Culhane had been the one facedown in the snow nearest the soddy. Munro didn't think that last precautionary round he'd had to put in old Kiowa's still form could have bothered him much, considering how many other times he'd been hit.

He dragged Culhane off the right-of-way, silently promising to try to live to give him that funeral. Munro left the two he remembered from the saloon where they lay. He scouted on to where the snow was trampled flat and wide by hooves and saw they went out in three directions at first. But Liz, circling wider, mounted, called out, "Over this way, Mingis." And when he remounted and rejoined her, he could see that, sure enough, the riderless ponies had gotten together for a powwow and headed northeast, in file, with one dragging its reins and lagging some, most likely from the way it had danced about to avoid stepping on the reins in the snow.

They followed the almost beeline trail over a few rises before Liz said soberly, "You can see where they're headed, can't you, Mingis?"

He said, "I can. I was hoping I was wrong. Thank God Miss June planned on staying in town tonight."

"I saw her at the Grange, earlier, with some other little snip. Why did you say you was hoping you was wrong? I find this surprising as hell, Mingis."

"It had to be somebody rich and important enough to sell stock in any numbers without arousing suspicion. Any small outfit like your'n or mine would be hard pressed to account for market beef wearing all sorts of odd brands. A man well established as a big dealer could say most anything, say, a tale of buying out small holders to save 'em the trouble of a long market drive."

Liz thought in silence as they rode on a ways. Then she said, "Fair is fair. Silas Dorman didn't sell no beef last roundup. I was there."

He nodded and said, "He couldn't have, this year. He was known far and wide as a horse trader. But he was already switching to beef. I sold him a few head of that Texas stock myself, and of course he'd already put his own brand on next to my trail brand. It's like I said, Liz. Nobody worries much about a big respected outfit selling stock that's been branded more than once. They all buy odd lots off smaller outfits to make up their market herds. Had they got away with that raid on the stockyards a while back, old Silas *would* have had a mess of beef to ship this year, from further down the rail line, of course."

She thought some more and said, "He'd still need friends in high places to pull anything as raw as that, wouldn't he?"

Munro nodded and said, "He's got 'em. He's a big shot in the Grange and one of the heads of the local party. That ain't saying every big Granger or Democrat in the territory is an outright crook. You just have to enjoy the trust and respect of the powers that be to get away with murder. So that's why he sent for them professional murderers. I kept messing up his plans, even before others started talking about running me for county sheriff."

She laughed uncertainly and said, "He should have stuck to marrying you up with his daughter. Do you mind if I ask how close that was, Mingis?"

He said, "He may have started out with that notion. I don't think he admired me so much after I started ruining his plans so regular. He must have been able to see that even as a son-in-law I was too honest to go along with his free-and-easy notions about property rights."

They topped a rise to see the snow-covered roofing of the

Dorman spread in the distance. All the windows were dark. But smoke was rising against the moonlight above the main house. He said, "Yeah. Them ponies made it back all right, and they remember what I told young Bob Westwood about dousing all the lights and sitting tight."

She said, "I don't think June Dorman knows anything about it."

He sighed and said, "There must be some logic to she-male logic, but I'll be whipped with snakes if I can figure out how that could matter, right now."

She said, "I can't say I like the stuck-up little sass, with her grand airs and notions of college and all, but it's still going to hurt her more than she deserves to be hurt if we expose her father as a damned old stock thief, Mingis."

He said, "I know. I feel sorry for her, too. But there's no way to let him off, even if we wanted to. A man who'd steal stock from his neighbors is bad enough. But a man who'd pay to have a neighbor gunned is just too ferocious to have running loose. This is more than personal, Liz. I can't be the only honest man in Wyoming. There's no telling who might wind up dead if I don't put a stop to this business. So here's what we got to do. I'm fixing to circle around, cut the house off from the stable, and keep 'em pinned whilst you ride for Lefty and the others, hear?"

She started to argue. He told her not to and spun the big blue to retreat from the rise and lope east out of sight from the Dorman spread. When he figured he had to be east of the layout, he swung north again, topped the rise, and saw that sure enough he was well southeast of the rooftops, facing the back wall of the long low-slung stables the old horse trader had put up.

He knew horses tended to howdy one another. So he dismounted a quarter mile off, stomped the reins into the snow, and hoped the big blue would have sense enough to stay put. Then he made sure there was a round in the

146

chamber of his Winchester and moved in the rest of the way afoot.

It wasn't easy. Since it wasn't a true winter night, the snow was already starting to crust. He was sure he sounded louder than a mean little kid busting windows in an alley as he came crunching across the open moonlit whiteness without a bit of cover to either side. But then he was up against the sod wall of the stable, trying not to breathe so loudly, and so far so good.

As he eased along the stable wall, searching for a gap, he grinned wolfishly and muttered to himself, "They're too shorthanded to watch every approach, and they'd naturally expect us to come in along them pony tracks on the far side."

He slid into a dark slot, eased deeper, and saw he was now facing the rear of the main house across the snow-covered backyard. That one door had to lead out of the kitchen where he'd had coffee and such a friendly conversation with pretty little June Dorman so long ago, when he'd still thought the world was run on the level.

He grimaced, hunkered down, and waited, covering the kitchen door with his carbine. He didn't look forward to facing Miss June after gunning her father. He hoped Liz could get back with help before he had to. Charging the house alone would be suicide. But as long as they couldn't get out to their ponies, they were as good as jailed, so what the hell.

He started to fumble for his pocket watch. He decided not to. He doubted he could read the dial in this tricky light, and even if he could, help would get here when it got here. Knowing what time it was, before anything happened, wouldn't change anything.

Liz would be back with help in time or she wouldn't. The boys he'd sent her to fetch would be able to handle the bunch in the house or they wouldn't. It was impossible to say just how many were holed up inside. Munro knew old Silas had laid off some of the hands he'd hired to handle horseflesh for him before he'd lost his remount contract with the army. But he'd hired some since that he said were cowhands. Whether they were or not, by this late date they had to know they were working for an old skunk.

Munro thought hard, trying to count the unfamiliar faces he'd had pointed out to him in town as riding for Dorman. But he just couldn't decide if they numbered four or six. He had to assume there could be more in there right now. Kiowa had said he'd come to town with only two backup guns, and they were accounted for. But there was no saying how many cow thieves Dorman had directly on his payroll and how many could be working as part-time sons of bitches.

Munro froze and felt his heart skip a beat when the back door across the yard popped open and a figure popped out like a cuckoo-clock bird to yell, in Silas Dorman's voice, "Hey, Slim? What's keeping you out there so long?"

Munro was sincerely glad he hadn't moseyed closer to the back of the house, when another voice called back from the outbuilding to his right, explaining, "Had to make sure them ponies was rubbed down good after all that time they spent playing in the snow, boss."

Dorman replied, "Well, get a move on and get back in the house with your gun, Slim. For unless we get lucky and it snows some more this side of sunup, eight guns ain't going to be enough!"

Munro grinned wolfishly in his hiding place and resisted the impulse to thank the old fool out loud. For he knew now that once Liz got back with his own pals, they'd be able to keep a gang that size pinned down until . . . what?

There was no way to capture the gang without help from town, and poor June Dorman was going to be mighty upset if the final result was vigilante justice at the end of a throw

148

rope. If her no-good skunk of a father had the common sense it took for serious dishonesty, he'd be riding right now and not denned up like a lobo who had to know he'd been tracked down.

Munro glanced up at the sky. More stars than anyone could count in one night were winking down from a now-cloudless sky. But it was early yet. If it stayed clear, the rascals in the house would surely make a break for it before dawn. It was their only chance. If Dorman had a lick of sense, he'd be packing right now and planning to send for his daughter from, say, Chicago. Miss June had been saying she liked it better back east in any case.

Munro settled down to wait some more for Liz and the others. Then he heard her, far away on the far side of the house, but it was still her voice, shouting, "You in the house! We got you surrounded, and we know what you done! Toss out your guns and follow 'em with your hands full of moonbeams, and I promise you a fair trial. Do we have to take you the hard way, there's no telling how my boys are likely to treat you!"

Munro scowled and muttered, "What boys, damn it? She ain't had *time* to get anywhere and back!"

Someone in the house must have thought she was bluffing, too. On the far side, there was the sound of breaking glass and the muffled squib of a rifle going off inside. The wrangler who was still in the stable ran across Munro's line of vision, fumbling for his six-gun as his chaps flapped a cloud of moonlit sugary snow in his wake. Munro was after him like a shot, and as they both reached the back door almost as one, Munro raised his carbine and planted a perfectly executed horizontal butt stroke in the nape of the owlhoot's neck. Slim's body slammed face first against the kitchen door and burst it inward. Munro leaped over his victim into the darkness, hooked the corner of the infernal kitchen table with one upper thigh, and spun around and

149

down into a crouch against the warm cooking range with his gun muzzle trained on the dim outline of the doorway beyond as much by luck as design.

But it was just as well he was low and to one side as the far doorway filled with a figure firing blindly across the dark and out the open back door at whomsoever. Munro's first .44–40 slug folded the wilder shootist at the waist like a jackknife and sent him flying back into the main sitting room.

Then Munro was up and charging forward through his own as well as the other man's thick gunsmoke. He ran in a crouch, of course. He still lost his hat as he tore out of the kitchen, doing some wild firing of his own, and crabbed sideways along the wall toward the fireplace and chesterfield he remembered from his more sociable last visit. He saw the man who'd shot his hat off fly backwards through the panes of a front window, mighty noisy, and dropped another like a bearskin rug in the dimly lit space between the big leather chesterfield and the banked hearth it was facing.

A six-gun flashed at him from a dark corner, almost parting the hair on his bare head as he fired back and dove headfirst at the chesterfield for cover. He hit too hard, and both he and the big sofa went over. As its back thudded hard on the floor, Munro just kept rolling and fired upward from a sitting position at the confused figures outlined above him by window and ruby hearth light until he noticed he didn't seem to have any more targets. He eased his tail along the length of the overturned chesterfield in the gloom, groping his way with his free hand on the rug. When it met a crumpled newspaper someone had left on the chesterfield seat earlier, he balled the paper up and tossed it into the fireplace. It caught fire on the coals and lit things up considerably as it flared. He was able to count four figures sprawled here and there in various states of bloody disrepair. He'd left one more out of sight by the back door, and one had gone through the window. So there had to be two left.

As the paper burned down, he rose gingerly to his feet and got out his six-gun for close work. From somewhere out in the night he heard Liz calling, "Mingis? Is that you making all that racket in there?"

He eased over to the nearest shattered window to call back to her, "Stay put and hold your fire! This house is still haunted a mite!"

He knew he was right when a door on the far side of the fireplace popped open and they both fired at the same time. Munro was luckier than the rascal who'd thought he had him located by the sound of his voice. The owlhoot fell back into the room beyond the fireplace with his boots on the door sill. Someone tried to shove the door shut, sobbing curses as the dead man's feet held it just ajar no matter how hard he shoved. He found out how dumb he was when Munro pumped three pistol rounds through the hardwood door at waist level and heard a strangled gasp, a horrible moan, and a dull thud.

Munro hunkered down in the dark, reloading, as he counted in his head. Then he nodded, rose to his full height, and moved in fast to kick the door wide open and fire down at both of the figures sprawled there at his feet.

Then he walked back to the front door, flung it open, and yelled, "Get in here, you fool woman. Don't you never do a thing you're told?"

He had to laugh, despite his mock anger, when Liz Standhope rose from the snow atop the rise west of the house like a frozen Venus from the waves, plastered white all down the front. She came down the slope stomping and cussing some. She waited until she could stomp harder on the front steps before she told him, "I don't have to do what any old man tells me. I am a free and independent woman of

151

means, and somebody has to look after you. You sure don't know how to look after yourself. What on earth made you rush in, lonesome, like that, you damned fool?''

He hauled her inside and slammed the door shut again as he told her, "A fool woman trying to get her fool tail shot off, I reckon. I thought I told you to ride for help.''

She said, "You told me. I never said I would. I had two good reasons. I knew they'd bust out if we gave 'em time to study on the fix them ponies put 'em in, and I thought we'd agreed to cover as much as we could for June Dorman. It's hard to keep family secrets even when two outsiders know about 'em. Dragging in more would have made it even harder. What have we got here, Mingis?''

He said, "I ain't sure. Let's get you out of that wet coat and shed some light on the subject.''

He helped her out of her long sheepskin and tossed it on the overturned chesterfield with their long guns. Then he moved to the fireplace, poked up the coals, and tossed some fresh logs on the grate. The results cheered the interior considerably, but as Liz gazed about she still said, "You sure are hell on the furniture. The rugs will never be the same, either. I know that one in yon corner. June Dorman introduced him to me in town the other week as a new hand her daddy had hired. Can't say I've met any of these other gents afore, though.''

He said, "The wrangler, Slim, is out in the kitchen. Partways at least. I reckon he was the last of the old crew. Honest horsehands don't make out so good as dishonest cowhands, I reckon.''

He bent over to haul the chesterfield upright so she could sit on it as he said, "I got two more in a back room to study." Then he reached for a candlestick above the fireplace and lit it. She noticed he still had his six-gun in his free hand and drew her own to follow him. He told her to stay back. But it was like ordering a wall around. So she was peering over his shoulder when he moved into the other room, holding the candlestick high, and though she didn't cuss as hard as he did, she sucked in her breath and said, "Oh, Jesus."

Caleb Norris lay dead in the doorway, staring up cross-eyed because of the way he'd been shot through the forehead. His gun lay on the rug at his side, and his brass badge was still pinned to his vest.

Beyond, crumpled in a ball at the foot of a bed covered with pink chenille, lay Silas Dorman, his gaping mouth still drooling blood on the pink shag rug. On top of the bed, with its back to the fluffed-up pillows and its long legs sprawled out, lay a big fancy-dressed rag doll with button eyes and a painted grin. Munro opined soberly, "This must be Miss June's room."

Then he moved over to check June's father's pulse. As he hunkered down, the more matter-of-fact she-male who'd come in with him stared down at a dressing table against the wall to note, "Well, it ain't true she uses French cheating paint like some say. Nothing here more treacherous than cold cream and lilac water. I reckon she's just a natural beauty, cuss her pretty hide."

Munro rose back to his feet, saying, "Dead as he'll ever be. He should have lit out while he had the chance. Or, better yet, never turned bad. I reckon once a man gets used to making big money regular, it drives him a mite loco to face going broke."

Liz said, "I reckon. Seeing he's in no position to say yes or no, do you reckon he'd mind if we had us some coffee to warm our innards afore we ride back to town with the tale?"

He agreed that was a sensible notion and led the way to the kitchen. He used the candle flame to light an oil lamp on the sideboard. Then he shoved what was left of Slim all the way out and shut the back door as Liz poked up the cook fire in the range.

As she got down the makings, she said, "You was right. He was living mighty fancy. Coffee in sealed cans, already ground, and look at all these other cans. Some all the way from Boston Town. What do you reckon caviar could be, Mingis?"

He said, "Fish aigs. I tried 'em once. They wasn't much. But they cost more than beans. I reckon some of the fancier notions originated with Miss June. She told me one time she liked to act sort of cultural."

Liz sighed and said, "I might have wound up more cultural if I hadn't had to start working for my keep so young. Sit down and I'll have our coffee ready directly."

He took a seat at the table, opening his own sheepskin wide so he wouldn't catch a chill riding back to town. As he watched Liz bustle at the range with her back to him, he said, "I don't think anyone will begrudge Miss June the value of this land, at least. It ain't as if her father stole all that much, you know."

Liz said, "I thought we'd agreed to shine as rosy a light as we could on this mess, Mingis."

He said, "I'd sure like to. But we got to tell everyone *some* damned thing about all the dead gents we left in our wake this evening, and anyone who can read sign at all won't have too much trouble putting it together the way it was."

She said, "Coffee will be ready in a minute," and came over to join him at the table, sitting across from him as she added, "You must not read sign as good as me, then. As *I* see it, the ringleader must have been that newcomer, Caleb Norris. He had to be a crooked lawman, working with the cow thieves."

"Liz, all them other gents lying on the rug with my hat out front was on the old man's payroll," Munro objected.

She said, "I ain't finished. They was no doubt taking advantage of him and his innocent daughter. When Caleb

Norris seen how good you was at messing up his devious plans, and don't forget everyone knows you and him was nominated for the same office, Caleb sent for hired killers to do you in. Only you done them in instead, and tracked their ponies here, smart as ever. As you rode in, the rascals made ready to gun you. No doubt they would have, had not poor old Silas tried to stop them, got kilt fighting such a band of desperadoes and treacherous help, and given you warning, at least, by getting his fool self killed like a hero."

Munro grinned across the table at her and said, "Remind me not to ever play checkers with you for money, Liz. But I still see some loose ends. For one thing, there's your tracks and—"

"I just got here, nosy woman that I am," she cut in, adding, "Do you reckon anyone's likely to suspect you took the eight of 'em on, lonesome, without no help at *all* from, say, poor old Silas Dorman? You sure must like to brag, Mingis Munro."

He laughed and said, "By damn, it ought to work. For when you study on it, I'd have no reason to be modest about gunning old Silas if I even suspicioned him for being a skunk who'd hired them killers to clean my plow. Nobody but a total lunatic would tell such a whopper for no reason, and since nobody knows our reason—"

"Don't you mean *your* reason?" she cut in, looking sort of wistful as she went on. "That June Dorman will stay rich as well as young and pretty. But at least I can be a good sport about it. What are you looking at so funny, you love-struck idjet?"

He reached across to take her hand as he told her, "A lady. I mean a real lady, Liz. But no offense, you're talking mighty dumb for such a smart old gal."

She said, "Pooh, let go my hand. I wouldn't cause a neighbor gal more pain than I had to, even if you wasn't so fond of her."

155

He kept hold of her hand. It was a windburned and work-hardened hand, but it still felt nice to hold. He said, "That's what I just said I liked about you. All but the part about me wanting to go chasing after that other gal. What in thunder would I do with June Dorman if I caught her, Liz?"

She raised a knowing eyebrow and said, "For openers, the gent is usually the one who gets on top. You think I ain't got eyes or even one looking glass at home? Everyone says she's your'n for the asking, and no man with a lick of sense would pass on a gal who's good-looking, rich, and even nice."

He chuckled fondly and said, "I reckon it takes a fool to know one, then. I got my own eyes, and the natural feelings of most men. But sooner or later what gets on has to get off and go about his chores. So then what? That pretty little gal couldn't even manage one herd, and we figure to be stuck with two betwixt us if they insist on voting me in as their sheriff."

She gasped, stared owl-eyed at him, then a tear ran down her cheek unbidden as she told him softly, "If that was meant the way I sure hope it was meant, my answer would have to be yes. But if you're just funning me, Mingis Munro, I mean to blow your fool head off!"

She sounded like she meant that.

And she was wearing a gun.